DMITRI
AND THE
MILK-DRINKERS

Michael Pearce was raised in Anglo-Egyptian Sudan, where his fascination for language began. He later trained as a Russian interpreter but moved away from languages to follow an academic career, first as a lecturer in English and the History of Ideas, and then as an administrator. Michael Pearce now lives in London and is best known as the author of the award-winning *Mamur Zapt* books.

ALSO BY MICHAEL PEARCE

The Mamur Zapt Series

The Women of the Souk
The Mouth of the Crocodile
The Bride Box
The Mark of the Pasha
The Point in the Market
The Face in the Cemetery
A Cold Touch of Ice
Death of an Effendi
The Last Cut
The Fig Tree Murder
The Mingrelian Conspiracy
The Snake-Catcher's Daughter
The Mamur Zapt and the Camel of Destruction
The Mamur Zapt and the Spoils of Egypt
The Mamur Zapt and the Girl in the Nile
The Mamur Zapt and the Men Behind
The Mamur Zapt and the Donkey-Vous
The Mamur Zapt and the Night of the Dog
The Mamur Zapt and the Return of the Carpet

The Dmitri Kameron Series

Dmitri and the One-Legged Lady
Dmitri and the Milk-Drinkers

The Seymour of Special Branch Series

A Dead Man in Malta
A Dead Man in Naples
A Dead Man in Barcelona
A Dead Man in Tangier
A Dead Man in Athens
A Dead Man in Istanbul
A Dead Man in Trieste

MICHAEL PEARCE

DMITRI AND THE MILK-DRINKERS

HarperCollins*Publishers*

HarperCollins*Publishers* Ltd
1 London Bridge Street,
London SE1 9GF

www.harpercollins.co.uk

First published in Great Britain by
HarperCollins*Publishers* 1997

This paperback edition 2017
1

A catalogue record for this book is
available from the British Library

ISBN: 978-0-00-825935-8

Printed and bound in Great Britain

MIX

Paper from
responsible sources

FSC™ C007454

1

Dmitri Kameron, Examining Magistrate, was walking along the corridor of the Court House when a woman came out of a door ahead of him.

'Help me, please!' she said.

Dmitri, a sympathetic young man fresh from law school and therefore lacking the consciousness of his dignity seen in the provinces as proper to his post, paused politely.

The girl was fair and well spoken; a bit above the run of women usually seen in Kursk, never mind the Court House, and Dmitri was impressed.

Later, he came to think he had been intended to be.

'Could you take me to the yard, please? I need some air.'

'Of course!'

He offered her his arm. Things, thought Dmitri, were improving.

'I felt faint,' she said.

'Oh, it's stifling in the Courtroom. They haven't caught up with the fact that it's spring yet. The heating's still going full blast. And then, of course, there are so many people.'

'I felt faint,' she said again.

'A breath of fresh air will put you right!'

But would she find it in the yard? There would be horse-shit everywhere, prisoners coming and going who, after long confinement, smelled worse than the horse-shit, the rank tobacco of the guards, and the dubious smell that came from the open drains. He had been meaning to speak about that to someone ever since he came, but the rooms used by the lawyers were at the front of the building and it was easy to forget what went on at the rear.

He stopped abruptly.

'I wonder – might it not be better if we went out by the front door? The air would be fresher. We could go for a walk in the park.'

And sod the case he was working on! They'd called the interval hadn't they? Well, they'd just have to wait.

'No, no, please! The yard!'

'Are you sure? I could – '

'Quite sure.'

She walked determinedly on.

In the yard it was as bad as he had feared. The carts had come for another convoy and their heavy wooden wheels had churned the usual mud of the yard to a deep bog into which the horses sank up to their fetlocks. The drivers were finding it impossible to turn the carts and everywhere men were shouting and swearing and there was a continuous spray of mud.

'Honestly – ' Dmitri began.

'I'll be all right. Really!'

He looked around for somewhere she could stand.

'This will be all right. Truly! But could you fetch me some water, please?'

He left her standing in the doorway while he went to find the water. There was a well in the yard, but he certainly was not going to wade across to that. He tried some of the rooms nearby and did indeed find a pail of water which might have been intended for drinking. But he couldn't find a cup and had doubts about the water anyway, so went on further. In the end he had to go all the way back to the lawyers' chambers at the front of the building before he could find a respectable cup and some trustable water.

When he came back he found her gone. It had taken him some time and no doubt she had got bored waiting. All the same he felt a little aggrieved.

'But you were the last person who saw her!' said Peter Ivanovich accusingly.

'Surely not. The ushers – '

He remembered now, however, that the corridor had been empty. All the courts had been in session and the ushers preoccupied with their duties.

'Someone in the yard – '

No one in the yard. Everyone very keen to distance themselves as far as possible. They had all been busy with the carts – Dmitri Alexandrovich had seen for himself – and had had no time to notice anything. Had Anna Semeonova gone into the yard anyway? When Dmitri Alexandrovich had last seen her she had been standing in the doorway. Was it likely that a decent, well-bred girl like Anna Semeonova would go out with all that filth, with all that language – Excuse me, Your Honour? A thick veil of mud lay over everything.

Well, it was unlikely, everyone had to admit. Far more likely that she had simply retraced her footsteps and gone out the front of the building, to get a breath of air in the park, perhaps –

'I suggested that,' said Dmitri.

'Well, there you are, then – '

Only she hadn't. Or at least the porters on the door swore blind that she hadn't.

'Do you think we wouldn't notice if a girl like Anna Semeonova walked out of the door?' they said indignantly. 'Truly, Your Honour – '

'Yes, but were you there, you oafs? Off for a drink – '

They denied this fervently; and, indeed, there was some independent evidence that they had been at their posts the whole of the morning. Had they just missed her, then?

'Anna Semeonova? A girl like that? Not a chance, Your Honour.'

The park? Had she been seen in the park? Was there anyone …? Yes, indeed, there were several people who had been in the park the whole time. Old Olga, selling sunflower seeds on her traditional pitch, Ivan Feodorovich sweeping the paths, a young clerk from the Court offices (and what was he doing out there? A woman, no doubt!) A woman it was, and she was produced, all tearful. Yes, Your Honour, she had been there all morning, well, not all morning, she was a respectable working girl, but just that part of the morning, only a few minutes, well, yes, the whole of the second half of the morning – it was such a lovely morning, Your Honour, quite spring-like – and she hadn't seen the young lady. Yes, she would have recognized her. She used to see her in the church. Such a lovely coat she would wear, fur trimmings on the lapels, white, black, white, black –

'For Christ's sake, shut that woman up!' said Peter Ivanovich with increasing irritation. Because he was getting nowhere. Incredible as it might seem, a respectable young woman, from one of the best local families, had simply disappeared. And, what was worse, she had disappeared from the Court House itself.

'It makes us look damned stupid,' the senior judge said to the Chief of Police. This was late in the afternoon and the girl had still not been found. They had searched the building not once but three times and were about to begin again.

'She must be here somewhere!' said the Chief of Police, Novikov. 'I mean, it stands to reason.'

'What would you know about reason?' said the senior judge sharply. Normally he got on quite well with Novikov. Indeed, when there was no one better available, he sometimes played cards with him. But that was probably a mistake. It encouraged

4

slackness. Give these people an inch and they would take a mile. Get off their backs for just one second and they were bloody useless.

And if anyone was bloody useless it was this damned man Novikov. You'd think anyone would be able to find a girl in a building if they set their mind to it. If they had a mind, that was. He gave Novikov a black look. Six hours! The girl had gone missing at about eleven o'clock and it was now past five o'clock. It would soon be dark. What if they hadn't found her by then? Her father was already here and was beginning to talk about the Governor. Well he didn't mind that too much. He was an old friend of the Governor himself. But Pavel Semeonov was also mentioning Prince Dolgorukov and that was different. Dolgorukov had influence in the places that mattered; not least in the Ministry of Justice, where the patterns of judges' careers were decided. Moreover, since the assassination of the previous Tsar and with the swing back to sterner measures, his power had grown sharply. He was definitely the coming man; and the judge, who had built his whole career on his talent for allying himself with coming men, was anxious to avoid a false step now. Especially over something as ridiculous as this!

Something must be done; and, since the population of Kursk seemed to be composed entirely of imbeciles and slackers, he would have to do it himself. He glanced at his watch. Six o'clock! He was due at Avdotia Vassilevna's in half an hour, but that would have to wait. He would miss the *zakuski*, which was a pity, for Avdotia Vassilevna had a flair for hors d'oeuvres. But sacrifices had to be made. He was damned, though, if he would miss the lamb cutlets; not for something as piffling as this.

He rang the bell on his desk. He would begin with that nincompoop who had, apparently, actually seen the girl, the only one, at any rate, in the whole of Kursk daft enough to admit he had seen her and then, the fool, somehow mislaid her.

'Fetch Examining Magistrate Kameron,' he directed.

Dmitri had also had ideas about how he was going to spend the evening. This was Thursday and along with other intellectual exiles from the capital he normally foregathered at the house of Igor Stepanovich to discuss the contents of the latest national periodicals. Tonight they were going to discuss an article in the most recent number of the *New Contemporary*. The article was unlikely to be very contemporary by the time it reached Kursk nor the journal very new, having been passed around the members of the group until they had all read it; but, reading it, they felt they were in touch with the latest ideas that were swirling around the capital. This was important as otherwise in the provinces you soon felt quite out of things. It was especially important to Dmitri, who had absolutely no intention of burying himself in a hole like Kursk for any longer than he could help.

There was, too, an added attraction this evening. Until quite recently the group had consisted entirely of men. This was less out of principle – in the group they were all advanced thinkers and, now that emancipation of the serfs was out of the way, saw the emancipation of women as the next great step – than out of necessity. The fact was that there was a shortage of intelligent women in Kursk. This was not their fault, as Igor Stepanovich pointed out: it merely reflected the general lack of educational provision for girls. Given such provision, in a few years young women would be able to talk on equal terms with young men. Even in Kursk.

The point was well made, and conversation was moving on to the general question of what form the education of women should take when Pavel Milusovich's sister, Sonya, interrupted. The conversation was taking place in the family's drawing room. She said that education was nothing to do with it. She had not been to university, she pointed out, but surely no one would deny that she had twice the brains of her brother. This was all too evidently true, and the argument stalled for a moment or two. Why, demanded Sonya, should she be excluded from the meetings of the group?

'You're not being excluded,' said Igor Stepanovich. 'It's just that you wouldn't be happy if you came.'

'How do you know?' asked Sonya.

'You'd be on your own,' said Igor.

'So?' said Sonya.

Igor couldn't immediately think of a reply. Another of the group, Gregor Yusupovich, said that it wouldn't look good. Other people were not as liberated as they were and if she was the one woman in a group of men it would prejudice her chances of marriage. Sonya said that, on the contrary, she thought it would improve them.

'Anyway,' she said, 'why does there just have to be one?'

'We're back to where we started,' said Igor. 'You'd be all right,' he conceded, 'but the truth is there aren't any other – '

'How about Vera?' said Sonya.

'Vera Samsonova?'

'You can't say she's not educated. She studied at St Petersburg. And she passed her exams first time!' added Sonya maliciously.

'Yes, but would she come?' asked Igor, affecting nonchalance. 'She's always seemed to me – '

'I'll ask her,' said Sonya.

And had.

She would be there this evening. Dmitri had no great hopes. He had seen her from a distance. Tall. And thin. Flat as a board. Straight up, straight down. Front and back. Bright, no doubt. No one who had taken the Advanced Women's Courses in the Faculty of Natural History could be a fool. They had been about the only route by which women could qualify to be a medical doctor. You had had to be pretty bright to get in, and very bright to stay on, because the professors had deliberately made it hard to. There had been a lot of hostility towards the course, not just from the medical profession but from the university. And from the

Government. They'd taken the first chance they could to close the courses down, a casualty, like so many others, of the backlash against reform following the assassination of Tsar Alexander.

He had met some of the women once, although the course itself had been closed by the time he got there. Very determined, the women had seemed. In fact, that was the trouble. Too determined. They seemed to go through life with clenched teeth.

From what he'd heard, Vera Samsonova was a bit like that. Spiky. No soft edges. All the same, he had been mildly intrigued at the prospect of meeting her.

And now, just as he was putting on his hat and coat, this bloody fool of a judge wanted to see him!

'There are things', said the senior judge severely, 'that a young lady of good family should not see. And the Court House yard is one of them!'

'She wanted to see it!' protested Dmitri. 'She was going there anyway.'

'Could you not have diverted her?'

'I tried, but she insisted.'

'You should have tried harder.'

'She wanted a breath of air!'

'But why go to the back yard for it? Why couldn't you take her out the front? The park … the flowers …'

'There aren't any flowers yet. They've only just cleared the snow away.'

'The air is wholesome at least,' said the judge, irritated, 'and you couldn't say that was true of the yard.'

'She *wanted* to go there!'

'I find that hard to believe. Would any respectable young woman want to go there, knowing what she might see? No,' said the judge warmly, 'what she *wanted* was just a place where she could get some fresh air. You chose to take her to the back yard and therefore it is in considerable measure your fault.'

8

'Fault! She asked me to show her the way and I showed her!'

'She placed herself under your protection.'

'Nonsense! All she did was ask – '

'A young woman?' said the judge incredulously. 'Distressed? Sees what she takes to be a respectable young man? An official of the Court, no less? Asks – quite properly – for assistance? If that is not placing herself under your protection, I'd like to know what is!'

Dmitri counted to five before replying and then, as that did not seem to be working, to ten.

'I could quite reasonably have restricted myself to pointing out the way,' he said at last. 'In fact, I chose – '

'Ah!' said the judge triumphantly. 'Chose!'

'To walk along the corridor with her. No question of legal responsibility arises.'

'Her father,' said the judge grimly, 'is a friend of the Governor. He moves in high circles in St Petersburg. An intimate of Prince Dolgorukov. Through him he has access to the Tsar. And you think no question of responsibility will arise?'

Oh ho, thought Dmitri. So that's the way the wind's blowing!

'I refuse to admit any personal responsibility in the matter,' he said quickly.

'Much good that will do you!' said the judge cuttingly. 'Much good,' he added gloomily, 'it will do any of us.'

'Oh, come sir!' said Dmitri. 'Things are not as bad as all that! There is probably some quite simple explanation for the girl's disappearance. Met a friend, perhaps, and gone off for a walk – '

'In the dark?' asked the judge, looking out of the window. 'She'd have been back by now. No,' he said, shaking his head, 'we've tried all that. Checked on her friends, the shops, her hairdresser – '

'A friend she wishes to keep secret, perhaps?'

'A male friend, you mean?'

'Well – '

'No question of that. Her parents are adamant.'

'They would be,' said Dmitri.

The judge looked at him.

'You think it's a possibility?'

'A far likelier possibility than that it's anything to do with the back yard.'

'You think so?'

'Sure of it. How could there be?'

'Well, of course you're right. A young lady of respectable family ... how could there be? You must be right.'

'Turned round the moment she took a look at it, I would have thought. Walked straight back along the corridor.'

'You think so? But then – '

'There will be some simple explanation.'

'I hope you're right. I'm sure you're right.' The judge looked at his watch. Still time to get to Avdotia Vassilevna's for the main course. Even the fish, perhaps. He snapped it shut.

'I'll leave it to you, then.'

'Leave it?'

'As Examining Magistrate. Do keep me informed.'

'But I thought ... You said ...'

'Yes?'

'That I was party to the case. And therefore it would be improper for me to act as Examining Magistrate.'

'But you denied that you were party to the case. Didn't you? I'm merely accepting your word. For the time being.'

One way or another, thought Dmitri, the bastards always got you.

'Well, I'll leave you to get on with it. While the scent is hot.'

Dmitri made a last effort to retrieve his evening.

'Aren't we being premature, sir? I mean, is there a case? Surely it's just a matter of continuing with the search? The police – ?'

'Useless. That fool Novikov. No, I'd prefer you to be involved right from the start. Someone bright, with a bit of energy, someone – '

'Responsible?'

'Yes. Responsible. That's the word.'

Sitting alone in the little room the lawyers used as a workroom, Dmitri nursed his wrath. There was plenty of it to nurse; first, wrath against the judge, not just for landing Dmitri in it but also for the general things he stood for and Dmitri stood against: age, seniority, authority, power, privilege, the System; next, wrath against Kursk, which was such a hell of a place that no wonder everything went wrong in it; and, finally, against this silly girl who had got herself lost and mucked up Dmitri's evening.

By this time on a normal day the Court House would have been empty. Lawyers, witnesses, defendants would have long departed. The caretakers would have retreated on to their ovens. Only at the back, perhaps, the last wagon would be squelching through the mud, trying to reach the firm crunch of the hard-packed snow outside.

Tonight there were lamps in all the rooms and people scurrying about everywhere. Novikov was searching the building for the fifth or perhaps sixth time. The dilemma before Dmitri was this: should he assume that Novikov was incapable of doing anything properly, and therefore make a search of the building himself? Or should he take for granted that the girl had left the building long before and was now happily chatting in some comfortable parlour with her girlfriends or, more likely, otherwise preoccupied in some comfortable bed with her boyfriend? The second was obviously the case. The trouble was that if by any unlikely chance it was the first, and the girl was lying stuffed in some corner somewhere, and was later discovered, then it would look bad. It would look bad for the Court House and, more to the point, since the judge had nailed him firmly with responsibility for the investigation, it would look bad for him, Dmitri.

Search, himself, it would have to be, and, no doubt, while doing it he could find himself a glass of tea in the caretakers' room.

Novikov had had the idea before him. He looked up, glass in hand, as Dmitri entered.

'I'm making a personal search,' he said, warming his backside against the fire. 'You've got to do it yourself. You can't trust these buggers to do it properly.'

'How far have you got?' asked Dmitri. 'Just here?'

Novikov looked pained.

'The whole of the ground floor,' he said. 'Every nook, every cranny, every cupboard, behind every pipe, down every sewer. You need a wash-up after you've done that, I can tell you! Ever searched a sewer, Dmitri Alexandrovich?'

'Suits some people more than others,' Dmitri said coldly. He wasn't going to be put down by the Chief of Police of a place like Kursk.

Novikov shrugged and put down his glass.

'The top floor now! Would you care to accompany me? At least there won't be any sewers.'

Dmitri was forced to admit, after half an hour had passed, that Novikov knew his job, or this part of it at least. It wasn't intelligence, Dmitri decided; it was cunning. Perhaps experience, too. Experience enough to know when a thing mattered and when it did not, cunning to be able to read the mind of the brutalized peasants who provided the bulk of the criminals in Kursk. Dmitri had no such cunning, he knew. He had never met a peasant until he came to Kursk, although they formed two-thirds of the population of Russia. Dmitri was a city-dweller through and through. And that, if he could manage it, was how he meant to stay. The important thing was not to get trapped in the provinces. That was where experience came in, both the judge's kind of experience and Novikov's. The experience to know that this was a thing that people higher up would be interested in and take notice of, experience at covering your back. Dmitri was beginning to feel that he could have done with more experience of the latter sort.

'A glass of tea, Dmitri Alexandrovich?' suggested Novikov, when they had finished the floor.

Dmitri concurred silently. He had already made up his mind that he would not now search the ground floor himself. Such things, especially the sewers, were best left to the Novikovs.

'What are you going to do now?' he asked.

Novikov looked at his watch.

'Nine o'clock,' he said. 'Nothing more tonight. It's too dark. Tomorrow we'll search the grounds. Then the park. First thing, though, as soon as it's light, we'll have people go through the building again, before the courts open. We may have missed something, you never know. And you wouldn't want people to come in and find …'

'Indeed not.'

'But,' Novikov went on, 'I won't do it myself.'

'No?'

'I'll be in the back yard. I want to have a good look in the mud. Before the wagons start coming. Care to join me, Dmitri Alexandrovich?' he asked maliciously.

Not at first light but at a decent hour, Dmitri called on the Semeonovs and was shown into the drawing room. A few moments later the Semeonovs joined him.

'Dmitri Alexandrovich Kameron,' he said bowing. 'Examining Magistrate. At your service.'

'He looks very young!' said Olga Feodorovna, inspecting him critically.

'Yes, he does,' said her husband. 'I don't call that good enough! Is that the best they can do?' he demanded, looking at Dmitri. 'A man like me deserves something better. Peter Ivanovich at least!'

'Peter Ivanovich is, indeed, occupying himself with the case, although, of course, formally it is the Examining Magistrate – '

'Formally?' said Semeonov. 'What do I care about "formally"? Don't come the petty bureaucrat with me, you young puppy! What's your name?' he demanded threateningly.

'Kameron. As I have just told you,' said Dmitri, seething.

'Well, Mr Examining Magistrate Kameron, you can run back to the Court House and tell them I want to see somebody different on the case, someone a bit more senior! I call this an insult. I can see I'm going to have to have a word with someone higher up, not just in Kursk, either. Prince Dolgorukov – '

'Kameron?' said his wife, 'Did you say Kameron?'

'I did.'

'That is not a Russian name.'

'My God!' said Semeonov. 'Are they sending us foreigners now?'

'They are not,' said Dmitri, stung. 'My family has been Russian for two hundred years. My great-great-grandfather served the Tsar – '

'Kameron?' interrupted Olga Feodorovna. 'What sort of name is that?'

'Scottish. My great-great-grandfather – '

'Served the Tsar, you say? In what capacity?' interrupted Semeonov.

'He built the Tsarina's palace.'

'Yes, but what rank?'

'For his services he was admitted to the *dvorianstvo*.'

'Really?' said Olga Feodorovna.

'A rank which my family has been proud to retain!' said Dmitri, fired up.

And would have been prouder still if anything, money for instance, had gone with it.

'Well, now, look – ' began Semeonov.

'Dmitri Alexandrovich!' said Olga Feodorovna, putting out her hand and smiling sweetly. 'How kind of you to call! *Charmant*!' she said to her husband. 'But why haven't you been to see us

14

before?' she said to Dmitri. 'My daughter would so like – oh, my daughter!' she cried, collapsing in tears.

'Now, now, my dear – '

'Madam! Madam!' cried Dmitri, supporting her to a sofa. 'You must not give way! Don't assume the worst! I'm sure she's all right.'

'You think so?' whispered Olga Feodorovna, looking up at him through her tears.

'I am sure!' cried Dmitri, carried away.

'And you will find her?'

'I will find her! I promise you!'

'You will? Oh, Dmitri Alexandrovich!'

'I will search the park myself.'

'Oh, Dmitri Alexandrovich! You will stay to lunch, won't you?'

It would have been unsociable to refuse. And over lunch he learned some more about the strange girl who had sought his help in the Court House.

A sweet girl, charming. Dmitri could believe that. Tender, passionate. Good qualities, in Dmitri's view, especially in women. Serious – serious about what?

'She used to read,' said Olga Feodorovna.

And not your French romances, either! Or, at least, not just your French romances.

'Real books!' said Semeonov, nodding significantly. 'Thick ones!'

'On …?'

Hospitals, said Semeonov. Children, said Olga Feodorovna. The poor.

'Oh, yes,' said Semeonov. 'The poor.'

For some reason Dmitri began to feel depressed.

'And church,' said Olga Feodorovna. 'She used to go to church.'

'But stopped,' said Semeonov.

Stopped?

'A girlish whim!' said Olga Feodorovna.

When was this?

'About three months ago,' said Semeonov.

'I pleaded with her,' said Olga Feodorovna. 'I asked her to think how it would look.'

But she wouldn't be persuaded?

'Well,' said Olga Feodorovna, 'you know girls.'

Any reason?

'Doubts,' said Semeonov.

Doubts? What sort of doubts? Religious ones?

The Semeonovs wouldn't say that.

'She was having a difficult time,' said Olga Feodorovna. 'You know; girls.'

Dmitri hadn't the faintest idea what she was talking about.

'Moody,' said Semeonov.

'Well, yes,' Olga Feodorovna had to admit, you could say that. A passing phase, though. And didn't Dmitri Alexandrovich think that made young women more interesting?

Oh, yes, Dmitri was sure of that.

'I knew you would understand,' said Olga Feodorovna softly.

It was a pity Dmitri Alexandrovich had never met her.

Dmitri was sure about that, too. In fact, he couldn't think how it was that he had come to miss her.

'Well, she didn't get about much,' said Olga Feodorovna. 'I tried to encourage her to, but she preferred to stay at home.'

'Reading,' supplemented Semeonov.

'You see!' said Olga Feodorovna, making what had once been a pretty *moue*. 'Serious!'

Not many friends, then?

'Only a few,' Olga Feodorovna conceded. 'In the best families, of course.'

Men friends?

'Oh, Dmitri Alexandrovich! We're not like St Petersburg, you know!'

Nevertheless –

'Frankly,' said Semeonov, 'there's no one here you'd encourage her to meet.'

'Except yourself, Dmitri Alexandrovich,' said Olga Feodorovna, smiling.

'When you get on a bit,' said Semeonov. 'In your career, I mean.'

But had there been anyone particular? A *tendresse*, perhaps?

'Oh, Dmitri Alexandrovich!' said Olga Feodorovna roguishly.

'No,' said Semeonov shortly.

Servants came and cleared the dishes away. Over the coffee, Dmitri said:

'And what exactly was Anna Semeonova doing in the Court House yesterday?'

'A fad!' said Semeonov, frowning.

'A whim!' said Olga Feodorovna.

'But what …?'

'She wanted to see a court in action,' said Semeonov. 'Well, I ask you!'

'Such a serious girl!' said Olga Feodorovna.

'It's all these books she's been reading. I'm all for giving girls education,' said Semeonov, 'but you can go too far.'

'I told her we could receive the lawyers socially,' said Olga Feodorovna. 'Only that wasn't what she wanted.'

'She wanted to go and see,' said Semeonov. 'I fixed it up with Smirnov. I didn't want anything too … well, you know what I mean. She's only a young girl.'

'Smirnov?' said Dmitri. 'That would be contracts, then.'

'I thought that was safest. Nothing too juicy. Smirnov said that it would be so boring she'd never want to go again.'

'I see. So there was nothing specific she particularly wanted to see, it was just the working of the courts in general?'

'She wanted to see the working of justice, she said.'

In that case, thought Dmitri, why go to the Law Courts?

2

———

Dmitri considered the fact that she was a serious girl a major indictment. He knew what serious girls were like. Especially in Kursk.

Besides, with her parents' permission, he'd taken a look in her room and seen the books: heavy, figure-filled stuff and all in German. Dmitri felt guilty about German. Germany was where a lot of the most advanced social thinking was going on and as a committed Westernizer, he should have been keeping himself *au courant*. He found the German language, however – or, at least, the German language as written by heavy German academics – hard going. So, apparently, had Anna Semeonova. She had persevered, nonetheless. That was another thing that Dmitri held against her.

The books gave a clue as to the direction of her seriousness. She was not serious about novels, she was not serious about music, she was not serious about ballet. What she was serious about was society. Unless Dmitri was much mistaken, the poor girl had had a fit of politics coming on.

This threw a different light on things. It knocked on the head, for a start, Dmitri's favourite theory at the moment (Dmitri had a lot of theories, it was relating them to facts that was the

18

problem), namely, that Anna Semeonova had gone off with a boyfriend. Seriousness and sexuality were, in Dmitri's view, incompatible. Unless – the thought made him stop in his tracks as he trudged back to the Court House through the remnants of snow – unless having a boyfriend was itself a political act!

It might be. With parents like the Semeonovs, any daughter could be excused for turning to rebellion; and what better form could rebellion take than running off with an unsuitable boyfriend? It was a sort of inverse of the mother's position. Psychologically, thought Dmitri, this sounded right; or if not right, at least interesting.

He decided he would pursue the matter with Novikov when he got back to the Court House. He was already sure that the Chief of Police's searching would not uncover a body. Dmitri was an optimistic fellow at heart and found it hard to believe, in general, that anyone was dead.

And so it turned out, at least in so far as all the searching that morning, in the park, in the grounds, in the back yard and, again, in the building itself, had failed to produce a body.

'Of course you won't find a body,' said Dmitri confidently, 'because the body walked out.'

'Now, look here, Dmitri Alexandrovich – ' began the caretaker.

They were sitting in his room drinking tea. The room was right next to the entrance and he was always in it, always drinking tea, as he pointed out.

'No one gets in or out without me seeing them. What do you think I'm here for?'

Dmitri had often wondered but wisely refrained from the comment.

'Your attention might have been distracted,' said Novikov.

'In that case Peter Profimovich would have noticed. Wouldn't you, Peter Profimovich?' said the caretaker, turning to his assistant.

Peter Profimovich grunted.

'There you are!' said the caretaker. 'One of us always keeps an eye on the door.'

Peter Profimovich grunted twice.

'And we would certainly have seen anyone like Anna Semeonova,' translated the caretaker, 'because girls like Anna Semeonova don't go in or out of this door very often.'

'It was a cold day,' said Dmitri. 'She might have been well wrapped up.'

'Dmitri Alexandrovich!' said the caretaker, shaking his head pityingly. 'Do you think we wouldn't have seen a figure like that? No matter how it was wrapped up?'

Peter Profimovich grunted three times.

'In any case,' said the caretaker, 'there wasn't much on yesterday morning and we remember everyone who went through. There was young Nikita, going out to see that girl of his – we always know it's getting on towards lunchtime when we see her appear at the gate of the park. There was Serafim Serafimovich going out for his usual drink – that was about eleven o'clock. There were a couple of clerks going to fetch things for Peter Ivanovich. There was a woman – '

'Ah!' said Dmitri and Novikov. 'A woman!'

'Who wasn't a bit like Anna Semeonova.'

'Disguise?' hinted Dmitri.

'She'd have to disguise her height as well,' said the caretaker caustically. 'She was about half the height of Anna Semeonova. And her hair. Anna Semeonova is a true blonde, a real Russian, you might say, whereas this girl's hair was as dark as a Tatar's. Which is not surprising,' said the caretaker, 'since that's what she was.'

Peter Profimovich laughed.

Dmitri refused to be put off.

'You saw her face?'

'We certainly did. Both of us. That's right, isn't it?' he appealed.

Peter Profimovich grunted.

'Cheekbones and all,' said the caretaker. 'If she was Anna Semeonova then I'm Tsar of Russia!'

'You watch out!' said Novikov. 'We don't want that kind of talk!'

'Saving His Reverence!' added the caretaker, crossing himself automatically.

'Anyone else?' demanded Dmitri.

'I've checked them all,' said Novikov seriously.

'She must have gone out the back, then,' said Dmitri.

'Dmitri Alexandrovich!' The caretaker bent over, convulsed. 'Forgive me, Dmitri Alexandrovich, but you don't know what you're saying! There's mud a foot deep – '

'I saw it!' snapped Dmitri.

'There's guards on the gate, there's soldiers everywhere. And then there are all those brutes! A respectable girl like Anna Semeonova? Forgive me, sir, you've got to be joking!'

'She couldn't have gone through the gate,' said Novikov positively. 'The guards would have seen her.'

'And don't tell me they wouldn't have remembered!' said the caretaker, with a knowing wink at Peter Profimovich.

'Shut up!' said Dmitri. 'Well, I don't know how she did it,' he said to Novikov, 'but I'm sure that's what she did. Because what else could have happened?'

'It's true,' admitted Novikov, 'she's got to be either here or not here.'

'She's somewhere else,' said Dmitri. 'And almost certainly with someone else. Which brings us to the question of friends. I've been talking to her parents and got a list.'

He showed it to Novikov.

'You're the Chief of Police. Where would you suggest I made a start? I'm looking especially for a political connection.'

'Political?' said Novikov doubtfully. He looked at the list. 'I don't think you'll find that any of these are what you might call political. They're all quite respectable.'

And that was basically the problem with Larissa Philipovna. She would have been so much happier talking about ponies than about politics. She seemed to Dmitri to be unbelievably young. How she could be an intimate of someone as poised and elegant as Anna Semeonova (who was improving all the time in his recollection), Dmitri could not think. If the image that Anna Semeonova had left with him was that of an ice-cool nordic heroine, the picture that her friend presented was that of a puppy in pigtails.

She received him, perched anxiously on the edge of her chair, in what her mother irritatingly referred to as 'the salon'. Oh, yes, (wide-eyed) she was Anna Semeonova's friend, her very closest friend. They saw each other all the time. They visited each other's houses almost every other day. Or used to. They wrote verses in each other's albums. Would Dmitri Alexandrovich care to …?

Dmitri winced and handed the book back.

Used to?

Well, yes. Just the last week or two, or perhaps it wasn't even weeks but months, they hadn't seen *quite* as much of each other. Anna Semeonova was studying.

Studying? What?

Books. Larissa Philipovna lowered her voice. This was serious; indeed, possibly more than serious: grave. Terribly difficult ones. She had shown some to her once and Larissa Philipovna had not been able to understand a word. Even Anna Semeonova herself had found them difficult. She had said so.

Then why had she taken to reading them?

Oh, it was because she was so very clever. She wanted to know about things. And why things were the way they were.

Politics?

Politics! Larissa Philipovna was aghast. No, no, definitely not! Anna Semeonova wasn't that kind of girl, not that kind of girl at all! Larissa Philipovna was sure –

'All right, all right,' said Dmitri. 'I just wondered. Now, tell me, was there anyone she liked to talk to about all the reading? Any new friends, perhaps?'

Well, there was that new doctor, Vera Samsonova –

'Ah, Vera Samsonova?' said Dmitri, pricking up his ears.

She had gone to her once to ask her about something in a book she had been reading.

'Something medical?'

'It was to do with numbers,' said Larissa Philipovna hesitantly.

Ah!

'The Health Question?' Larissa Philipovna put forward, emboldened.

'I see. And Anna Semeonova called on her, did she?'

'Yes. And she was very nice. She told her everything she wanted to know and a lot more besides. And she said she could come again if she wanted. And I think she *did* go again. Only ...'

'Only what?'

'Only I don't think that makes Vera Samsonova a *friend*, does it, Dmitri Alexandrovich? Not a *real* friend, the way Anna and I are friends? I mean, she's so much *older*. She couldn't be, could she?'

Blue eyes looked up trustingly at Dmitri.

'Not a real friend,' said Dmitri, and immediately kicked himself. Why had he let her wheedle that out of him?

'I know,' breathed Larissa Philipovna.

'There are different kinds of friendship,' he said sternly.

'Oh, yes!' said Larissa Philipovna.

This examination was not going the way he had intended.

'Tell me about her friends,' he said firmly. 'Did she have a boyfriend, for instance?'

'Oh, Dmitri Alexandrovich!' she cried, and collapsed in a fit of giggles.

The door at the end of the room opened slightly. It was that bitch of a mother, he was sure.

Nettled, he moved closer to Larissa Philipovna. She was not altogether unattractive. Or, at least, she wouldn't be in about ten years' time. Physically, that was. Mentally, of course …

'Dmitri Alexandrovich!'

'Would you care for some tea, Dmitri Alexandrovich?' said the bitch of a mother, coming definitely into the room.

Vera Samsonova, tracked down at last to the small room she used as a dispensary, regarded him unwelcomingly.

'Yes?'

Dmitri declared himself.

'I'm sorry I missed you last night,' he said.

'You didn't miss me. I didn't go.'

'I thought that Sonya – '

'She asked me. I wasn't free.'

'Oh.'

'In any case, I probably wouldn't have gone.'

'Oh, that's a pity. Why not, may I ask?'

'I think such gatherings are a bit beside the point,' said Vera Samsonova. 'Don't you?'

'Beside what point?' asked Dmitri cautiously.

'If you're looking for intellectual involvement you're not going to find it there.'

'Oh, I don't know. The people are very agreeable – '

'Agreeable,' said Vera Samsonova, 'but not very interesting.'

'Considering that we live in Kursk – ' Dmitri began.

'It's not where they live,' said Vera Samsonova, 'it's the kind of people they are. Dilettante. And naturally they want to talk about dilettante-ish things.'

'Art?' said Dmitri, annoyed. 'Culture? Where Russia is going?'

'Perhaps the subjects are not dilettante,' Vera conceded. 'It's just the way they are talked about.'

'Ah, well, there I agree with you – '

'In terms of generalities. You ask where Russia is going; not what it ought to be doing about sewage.'

'Sewage!'

'Yes, sewage. And farming and engineering and taxation – '

'Taxation!'

'Taxation.'

'Boring!' said Dmitri, rallying.

'Real!' said Vera Samsonova defiantly.

'Absolute nonsense!'

'You see?' said Vera. 'Prejudiced!'

'Not prejudiced at all,' said Dmitri: 'rational. And surely these things can be discussed rationally. That's the point of our gatherings.'

'You've got the wrong people there,' said Vera. 'You ought to have surveyors and agronomists – '

'Sewage experts?'

'Certainly.'

'You'll be saying doctors next!'

Vera considered. Then, unexpectedly, her face dimpled and broke into a smile. Up till now, Dmitri had attributed to her all the charm of a pair of scissors.

'Well, perhaps not doctors. At least, not the kind of doctors we have in Kursk!'

'There you are! Come and give us a chance to argue your points.'

'Maybe. It would certainly be better than arguing them here. Now, look, I've got work to do. Haven't you?'

'I'm doing it,' said Dmitri, injured. 'I'm here on business.'

'You are? Well, it's a pretty relaxed kind of business compared with mine, I can tell you. Or perhaps it's just that our approaches are different. You prefer a more general one. What was it exactly that you came for?'

'I came to ask about Anna Semeonova.'

Vera Samsonova put down the burette she had been holding and turned to give him her full attention.

'Has she been found?'

'Not yet.'

'Well, I suppose that's good news in a way. I was afraid – ' she gave a slight shake of her shoulders – 'that the next time I might see her was when she was brought here.'

'Do you have any particular reason for fearing that?'

'No.'

'She might just have run away.'

'She might.'

'If she had, would that surprise you?'

'Would it surprise me?' Vera Samsonova considered. 'No, to the extent that she is an independent girl and capable of independent action. Yes, to the extent that she would have had to have had a reason.'

'And you don't know of one?'

'No. Was there one?'

'I don't know. That's why I'm asking you.'

'Well, I'm not the person to ask. I only know her slightly. She's come to see me once or twice recently to ask me about something that she's been reading.'

'Which was?'

'Oh, it was a book about infantile mortality. A bit out of date. But there were some comparative statistics she couldn't understand – not the numbers, but the medical terms used.'

'Nothing political?'

'Political?' Vera Samsonova stared at him.

'Well, I just wondered. She disappeared from the Law Courts, you see, where she had been to watch a case being tried, and I wondered what had taken her there. Her parents thought mere idle curiosity, but I wondered …'

'What did you wonder, Dmitri Alexandrovich?'

'If it was an interest in justice.'

'And that makes it political?'

'Sometimes.'

Vera Samsonova was silent. Then she said:

'We did not talk about that, Dmitri Alexandrovich. We talked about medical terminology. But, yes, in so far as the terminology was to do with perinatal mortality and the statistics were to do with comparisons between Russia and other countries and between rich cities like Moscow and poor ones like Kursk, yes, questions of justice were implicit, and, yes, if you press the questions far enough they do require answers which in the end are political. Was that what you wanted to ask me, Dmitri Alexandrovich? Because if it was, you've had your answer and now I suggest you leave.'

'Don't get annoyed!' said Dmitri.

'Well, I *am* annoyed, because it sounds as if you're trying to get me to incriminate myself.'

'I'm not,' said Dmitri. 'It's just the way lawyers talk. Or, at least, Examining Magistrates talk.'

'It's the assumptions that lie behind what you say!'

'I'm not assuming anything. I'm trying to find out what happened to Anna Semeonova. At first I thought something dreadful must have happened. But if it had, I think by now we would have found the body. So perhaps she went off of her own accord. But why and where to? Or, rather, *who* to? A boyfriend? But everyone assures me that is not so. Some other friend, then? We have been round them all. And in the end, Vera Samsonova, I have come to you.'

'I hardly count as a friend.'

'That will be a relief to Larissa Philipovna. But since it is clear that Anna Semeonova did not come to you, it means that we have once again drawn a blank, in that respect at least. But perhaps you can help me in another way. I ask myself why she could have gone off. Now, you and everyone else say that she is a serious girl; and she was at the Law Courts. Might there not be a connection between that and her disappearance?'

'Why did you ask me about politics?'

'Because that could be the connection.'

'You think she has run off to be a revolutionary?' said Vera derisively.

'Well, young people from good families do sometimes go off these days. Not to become a revolutionary but to work for a cause. Giving out literature, addressing meetings, organizing with others – '

Vera Semeonova shook her head.

'Anyone less likely to become a political activist than Anna Semeonova,' she said firmly, 'you never saw. For that kind of thing you require a degree of hardness, perhaps, even a degree of hate. Anna Semeonova wasn't like that at all. She was a sweet, gentle girl, full of sympathy for others.'

'All right,' said Dmitri, 'perhaps I've got it wrong. I don't know the girl, I've hardly even spoken to her. Let me try something else on you; you said she was full of sympathy for others. Is it possible that she could have gone off in some daft quixotic way to work for the poor? In a monastery, perhaps – no, not monastery, her parents said she'd gone off the Church, but something like that?'

'A sort of personal "Going to the People"?' asked Vera, interested.

She was referring to the great movement of some years earlier which had sent hundreds of idealistic young people out into the countryside to work for the improvement of the poor; an initiative that the poor had not universally appreciated.

'That sort of thing,' said Dmitri, who had sided with the poor on this matter.

'She said nothing to me,' said Vera.

'Oh, well …'

But Vera was thinking.

'It's a long shot,' she said, pulling a prescription pad towards her, 'but I can give you the name of a family. I mentioned them to her once – it was the last time she came – when we were talking about the way in which conditions contribute to infant mortality. You know, drunken father, ignorant mother, poverty, dirt, dozens of children already. Anna could hardly believe some of the examples I gave. She asked if there was anyone I knew whom she could go and see, so I told her about the Stichkovs. She wouldn't come to any harm, the man is always unconscious and the woman is warm and kindly, quite motherly, really, in fact, far too much so – '

Dmitri felt oppressed by the sheer fecundity. One babe was at Mrs Stichkov's breast, two, hardly bigger, at her feet. Elsewhere in the room there appeared to be three more infants and there were certainly at least two outside. From time to time one of the children at her feet hauled himself up Mrs Stichkov's skirt and applied himself to her free breast.

'It's food, after all,' said Mrs Stichkov, 'and there's not much of that about with Ivan not working.'

Ivan was certainly not working. He was stretched on his back in a far corner of the room snoring loudly. Even at this distance, Dmitri could smell the vodka.

'He doesn't work much,' Mrs Stichkov acknowledged.

Except, thought Dmitri, when he roused himself to perform his conjugal duties, which appeared to be pretty frequently.

'Not since he's hurt his back,' supplemented Mrs Stichkov.

'Ah, he's hurt his back?'

'Carrying the loads. He can't carry a thing now. Not even the water. You need a man for that, the buckets are that heavy! Anna Semeonova tried to help me once, but she couldn't even lift the pail, not when it was full. You need a man, really, and she's just a slip of a girl.'

'She tried to help you, did she?'

'Yes, Your Excellency. She said, "It's not right, not with you expecting and all." But I said, "Lots of things are not right, and if I don't do it, who will?" "I will," she said, and she tried, but, bless her, she couldn't even lift it. "You look after Vasya", I said, "and I will do it." "It's not right," she said, "not with your time

29

so close," and she just stood there. And then Marfa Nikolaevna came along and said, "No, it's not right. That idle man of hers ought to do it, but he won't lift a finger." She's got a sharp tongue, that woman has. "I'll find someone, Mrs Stichkov," she said. And off she goes and comes back with one of the men from her place. Mind you, he wasn't that much better than Anna Semeonova, nor much bigger, neither, not with him being a Jew. Still, what do I care about that. I said to Ivan, "At least he gave me a hand, which is more than can be said for some people – "'

Mrs Stichkov shifted the baby from one breast to the other, gently detaching the other child as she did so.

'– And then he gives me a cuff!' she said cheerfully. 'I don't mind, it's not much of one – he can hardly stand up, he's that drunk – but Anna Semeonova gets very angry. I can see she's going to say something, so I say quickly: "Don't mind him, love, it's just his way!" But she doesn't like it, I can see that, and she goes out, and a little later I hear her talking to Marfa Nikolaevna. Which is all very well, I'm not saying that the woman is wrong, but you have to watch out with her. Sometimes it's better to let things rest easy. But she won't, you see, she's always got to out with it, and when it's man and wife, it doesn't pay to meddle.'

Over in the corner, Ivan moved loudly. Mrs Stichkov looked at him lovingly.

'You don't always know what a marriage is like,' she said, 'not from outside. Especially not if you're a single woman. "What does she know about it?" I say to Anna Semeonova. But Anna Semeonova stands there cold and unforgiving. "You're too forgiving, Mrs Stichkov," she says. "Sometimes those outside can see better." But then, she's another, isn't she? Single?'

'I believe so,' said Dmitri.

'She won't be for long,' said Mrs Stichkov. 'Not a girl like her. So pretty! A real Russian! And rich, too. Or so Ivan says. "Stay on the right side of her," he says, "and it'll be worth a rouble or two."'

'She's never said anything about having a boyfriend, has she?' said Dmitri, still diligent to eliminate options.

'Boyfriend?' Mrs Stichkov chuckled. 'She's not found out yet what it is men carry inside their trousers! A real innocent! "And it's best if she stays like that," I said to Marfa Nikolaevna, "so don't you go putting any of your ideas in her head!"'

'What sort of ideas?' said Dmitri.

Mrs Stichkov looked vague.

'Ideas,' she said.

Dmitri tried again.

'This Marfa Nikolaevna,' he said, 'what sort of woman is she?'

'She's got a sharp tongue. Everyone knows that! There's hardly anyone who's not felt the rough edge of her tongue at some time or another. That's why it is no one will have her. And that, of course, only makes her sharper. "It'd be a blessing," I say to Ivan, "if some man would take that girl down in the fields some time." "Well, no one's going to do that," says Ivan, "not unless it's one of her own kind." You'd think one of them would, wouldn't you? She's not bad-looking.'

'What are these ideas you say she has?'

'It's not ideas,' said Mrs Stichkov, 'it's what she says!'

'And what does she say?'

'Oh, about the land and all that.'

'What about the land?'

'She says it oughtn't to be owned by anyone. "You can't have that," I said, "that's silly. You can't just leave it lying around!" "No, no," she says, "that's not it. Everyone would own it together, it would belong to everybody." "The peasants wouldn't like that," says Ivan. "They think it should all belong to them." "That's because they don't know any better," she says. "Well, you go and tell them that," says Ivan, "and see where it gets you!" "That's just the trouble," she says; "people won't listen! And because they won't listen, the rich can get away with anything." "You want to watch that kind of talk, my girl," says Ivan, "or else you'll be in

31

trouble." So then she shuts up, she knows she's gone a bit too far.'

'Was that the kind of thing she was talking about with Anna Semeonova?'

'She just talks,' said Mrs Stichkov. 'Out it all comes! Just like mother's milk,' she said, looking fondly down at the baby, now replete and blotto on its mother's lap.

The houses were on the edge of town and just beyond them were open fields, still white with snow, and occasional clumps of birch trees, their branches heavy with ice. Dmitri contemplated the prospect and shuddered. Not for him the great open space of Russia, the steppe that poets sang about; for him the great open boulevards of St Petersburg, and that was exactly where he meant to be as soon as he could escape from this dump.

Back up to his left was a tanner's yard and the smell of the yard hung over the whole area. The acrid fumes irritated his eyes and caught at his chest in a way that he did not understand until he saw the empty drums piled at the tannery gates. Chemicals were used in the yard's processes. Little yellow rivulets ran down from the yard into the fields, colliding on the frozen surface of a small stream. Further along the stream the ice was broken and ducks, strangely discoloured, were swimming. Further along still, two women were filling pails to take up to their houses. Was this where Mrs Stichkov came to fetch her water? Where Anna Semeonova had tried to help her?

Of an impulse he went over to the two women. They put down their pails and watched him approach: a visitor from Mars.

'I wonder if you could help me,' he said, saluting them. 'I'm trying to find Marfa Nikolaevna's.'

They looked at him rather oddly. Then one of them gathered herself.

'The tailor's is over there,' she said, pointing.

'Thank you.'

He looked down at the pails. The water in them was yellowish. And, now he came to look at it, everything was yellowish. The mud was yellowish, his boots were yellowish, the broken ice on the stream was yellowish, a duck clambered out and waddled towards him and that, too, damn it, was yellowish on its under-feathers.

'This water is not fit for drinking,' he said sternly.

The women shrugged.

'It's all the water there is, Your Honour,' said one of them.

'You should go up beyond the yard,' he said.

'It's much further,' said one of the women quietly.

'You should think of your children!'

'Lev Petrovich should think of our children,' said one of the women bitterly.

'Lev Petrovich?'

'He owns the yard.'

'Someone should speak to him.'

'Marfa Nikolaevna did,' said the woman, 'and see where it got her!'

'I will speak to him.'

'Thank you, Your Honour,' said the other woman. 'That may help.'

'It won't help,' said the first woman dismissively. 'He'll just take it out on us. Thank you, Your Honour,' she said to Dmitri. 'It's kindly meant, I know, but sometimes it's best to leave things alone.'

'Well, I'll see … and this Marfa Nikolaevna, you say, went to see him?'

'Yes, Your Honour.'

'And got nowhere?'

'She speaks too bitter,' said the second woman.

The other woman turned on her.

'Not this time. She spoke real civil. Agafa Sirkova was listening at the door and she said she couldn't get over how polite she was. Not that it made any difference. He threw her out just the same.'

'Her reputation went before her,' said the second woman. 'That was the trouble.'

'It would have been the same whoever had gone.'

'Well, that's very true, and that's why it's best to leave these things alone, as you yourself were saying to this gentleman only just now.'

'But Marfa Nikolaevna, I gather, was not one to leave things alone?' said Dmitri.

The first woman gave a little laugh.

'You could say that,' she said. 'Yes, you could certainly say that! She was a bit of a firebrand. She wasn't one of us, Your Honour. She came from the steppes. Those Tatars, they light up at anything.'

'Well,' said Dmitri, 'all this is not really my concern. I am hoping she might be able to help me on something else. The tailor's, you say?'

As he left, he was aware again that they were looking at him rather oddly.

The snow on this side of the stream, between the houses, had become a sea of mud, through which his boots squelched noisily. Great, discoloured puddles lay everywhere. Half in one of them, half out, he could see a rat lying on its back, its body still and contorted, its feet in the air, the underside of its belly tinged with yellow. The fumes from the tannery made him cough and reach for his handkerchief. This was definitely not the place for a young woman like Anna Semeonova; nor, frankly, was it much of a place for a promising young Examining Magistrate.

Dmitri pushed open the door and went in. The room was full of women sewing. It was so dark that he was amazed that any of them could see.

'I'm looking for Marfa Nikolaevna,' he said.

A man in a skull cap came forward.

'Marfa Nikolaevna?' he said, with a worried expression on his face. 'But, Barin, she is no longer here.'

'No longer here?'

'She hasn't been here for, oh, over three weeks now. Not since they came and took her away.'

'Where is she now?' said Dmitri harshly.

'Her case came up yesterday,' said the tailor, 'in the District Court at Kursk.'

3

The following morning, Anna Semeonova had still not been found.

'It's bad,' said Peter Ivanovich. 'First, because she's a nice girl. I've known her since she was six. At that time she looked like a dumpling and everyone was afraid she was going to take after her father. Recently, though, she has thinned out and is becoming a beauty like her mother. Second, because her father blames us. Thirdly, because so does everyone else.'

Dmitri was always irritated by the Presiding Judge's pedantic habit of enumerating his points.

'She did, after all, disappear from the Court House,' he pointed out.

'I know; very inconsiderate of her,' said Peter Ivanovich. 'Why couldn't she have disappeared from her home? We would still have been blamed, but we wouldn't have looked quite as stupid. And now I'm afraid they will send someone down from St Petersburg.'

'To take charge of the case?'

Dmitri wasn't sure that he liked this. It was his case; and thus far in his career he had not been assigned so many that he could afford to be blasé. This was, actually, if you included the ridiculous affair of the old woman and the cow, only his second case. And were they now going to take even that from him?

'We must resist,' he said sternly.

Peter Ivanovich looked at him pityingly.

'Tell me how you get on', he said, 'as Examining Magistrate in Siberia. Let me talk to you as a father, Dmitri Alexandrovich: obstruct, but do not resist. That is the first rule of bureaucracy. Besides,' he said, 'they won't take over the case. They will leave you in charge. So that you can be blamed if things go wrong. That is the second rule of bureaucracy: make sure that responsibility always lies elsewhere.'

The advice of a master, thought Dmitri. Peter Ivanovich was wrong, however. The first rule of bureaucracy was surely to keep your mouth shut; which Dmitri was grimly trying to do.

'The answer is, of course,' continued Peter Ivanovich, 'to solve the case yourself before they get here. How are you getting on, incidentally?'

He listened to Dmitri's account of yesterday's inquiries.

'Interesting,' he commented. 'Who would have thought it? A girl like Anna Semeonova – getting herself mixed up with such people!'

'I'm not sure how far she *is* mixed up with such people,' said Dmitri. 'That's one of the things I wanted to ask Marfa Nikolaevna.'

'Ask her, by all means,' said Peter Ivanovich generously, 'although I doubt if it will help you much.'

'I would if I could,' said Dmitri, frowning. 'But there's been a bit of a mix-up.'

'Another one?' said Peter Ivanovich. 'Oh dear! These people! What is it this time?'

'They can't trace her.'

'Come, come!' said Peter Ivanovich. 'She was in court the day before yesterday, wasn't she? And surely she was not acquitted?'

'Oh, no. She was sentenced, all right. It's what happened after-wards that's not clear.'

'It's as clear as daylight,' said Peter Ivanovich. 'She was a polit-ical prisoner, wasn't she? Then she would have been sent back to prison to await transportation.'

'So one would have thought. But the prison denies readmitting her. And there's a complication. Some of the prisoners that day were sent directly to join the Siberian convoy.'

'Well, perhaps that's what happened to her, then,' said Peter Ivanovich patiently.

'They've checked the lists,' said Dmitri, 'and they can't find her.'

'They've made a mistake. It's always happening. A clerical error. Either there or at the prison. Get them to check it again!'

'I have. There's no record in either place of a person of that name.'

'There must be! She must be either in the one place or in the other. Either in prison or in the convoy. She can't be still in the Court House, can she?'

'Well, no.'

'I mean, you've searched the place thoroughly, haven't you? For that other girl?'

'Novikov has searched the place,' said Dmitri, learning fast. 'Thoroughly, he says.'

'Well, then!'

'So she must be either in the prison or with the convoy. Unless …'

'Yes?'

'She's disappeared. Like the other one,' said Dmitri with emphasis.

'Oh, my God!' said Peter Ivanovich, clapping his hands to his head.

'If this woman has indeed disappeared,' said Peter Ivanovich coldly, 'I hold you responsible.'

'Me, Your Honour?'

The Chief of Police reeled back.

'You're responsible for security arrangements, aren't you?'

'Only in the Court House, Your Excellency! Only in the Court House!'

'But that's where she's disappeared *from*.'

'Ah, but did she, Your Honour?' said Novikov, recovering quickly. 'Did she? Perhaps she escaped as the carts were going back to the prison – '

'She's not on the carts list,' said Dmitri.

'Or from the convoy – '

'She's not on their list, either.'

'She must be! She must be!'

'What are these lists?' asked Peter Ivanovich.

'At the end of the sessions the Clerk of the Court prepares a list of all those sentenced,' said Dmitri. 'From it, an assistant clerk compiles two separate lists, one for the officer in charge of the prison carts, one for the officer in charge of the convoy. The prisoners are assembled in the yard and assigned to one set of carts or the other on the basis of the consolidated list. As they get to the carts their names are checked against those on the separate lists. Marfa Nikolaevna's name appears on the consolidated list, but not, so far as I can tell, and I've asked both the Prison Administration and the Convoy Administration, on either of the separate lists.'

'They must have made a mistake,' said Novikov.

'Exactly what I said!' said Peter Ivanovich.

'I got them to check,' said Dmitri.

'Ah, yes, Your Honour, but it will be different if I ask them. Saving Your Honour's presence, but they won't have bothered much for someone new like yourself. Let me have a word with them, Your Excellency,' said Novikov, turning to Peter Ivanovich, 'and I'll soon sort this out.'

'Do so; and don't take too long about it, either. One can't have people disappearing from the Court House. Really, one begins to feel quite nervous!'

Novikov returned, beaming, before the lawyers had finished their lunch.

'There you are, sir, what did I tell you? Sorted it out in no time! A simple mistake, sir, as you supposed.'

He put a piece of paper on the table before Peter Ivanovich and smoothed it flat.

'There you are, Your Excellency!' He pointed with a stubby forefinger. 'That's what you want!'

Peter Ivanovich adjusted his pince-nez.

'Is it?'

'I know, sir. You're having difficulty. And not just you alone, sir. Everyone else. That's how the misunderstanding arose. No one's fault, sir, except for that fat clerk who'll be feeling the toe of my boot up his fundament if he doesn't take more pains next time.'

Peter Ivanovich looked again.

'I suppose you're right,' he said doubtfully.

'Not convinced, Your Excellency?' Novikov chuckled. 'Well, that doesn't surprise me. In fact, it's what I told myself. An old fox like His Excellency will want something more than that, I said. And quite right, too! So I did a bit of nosing around and, as luck would have it, who should I come upon but young Stenka. Come in, lad!' he called out into the corridor.

A fresh-faced young soldier appeared hesitantly in the doorway.

'Come in, lad. His Excellency won't bite you. Now, you come in and tell His Excellency what you told me.'

The young soldier cleared his throat nervously.

'I was on the carts,' he began.

'That very afternoon,' interjected Novikov.

'Yes, right, that afternoon. The women's cart, as it fell out. Well, I don't mind that, I mean, you never know what you might see, and you're not going to have any trouble, are you? I mean, not any real trouble. They say things, of course, you've got to put up with that, but I know how to handle that. I just say: "You bloody shut up or you'll taste the butt of my gun!"'

'The cart, lad, the cart,' put in Novikov hastily.

'Yes, right, the cart. Well, there weren't many of them that afternoon, not women, I mean. Only a few for us. So I've got a bit of time, and I see this girl. A real Russian beauty, she is. Oh ho, I think, I'll bet you've got a nice pair of apples, and I give her a pinch as she goes by. Well, she jumps about half a verst. "What's your name my beauty?" I say. She doesn't answer, so I go to the sergeant and I say: "See that one there? What's her name?" "What do you want to know for?" he says. "A taste comes before a feast," I say. "Well," he says, "there's not going to be much of a feast for you, my lad, because she's going straight on to the main convoy and you're going to be stopping here." "Never mind that," I say. "What's her name?" He looks at his list. "Shumin," he says. "Marfa Nikolaevna Shumin."'

'Shumin?' said Peter Ivanovich. 'You're sure about that?'

'Pretty sure, sir. But I'm dead sure about the "Marfa". My own sister's named Marfa, it's a bit of a family name. "That's a good omen," I said to myself. "She's almost one of the family, like."'

Novikov looked at Peter Ivanovich.

'Satisfied, sir?'

'There seems no doubt about it,' Peter Ivanovich conceded.

'That's what I thought, sir, once I'd talked to Stenka. The name by itself, I said, won't be enough to convince Peter Ivanovich. But a witness, an honest witness – well, that's a different matter!'

'Happy, now?' said Peter Ivanovich, looking at Dmitri.

'Not very.' Something was troubling him. In what the guard had said. He dismissed it for the moment. 'This was the convoy, was it?' he said to Stenka. The soldier nodded. 'That means she's halfway to Siberia by now. How am I going to question her?'

'Not very easily,' said Peter Ivanovich. 'Unless you care to go after her.'

Novikov gave a great guffaw.

'That's a good one!' he said, nudging Stenka. The soldier, not entirely understanding, but dutiful, joined in.

Peter Ivanovich allowed himself a slight smile.

'I'm afraid our young colleague is one for the psychological,' he said.

'Psychological, Your Excellency?'

'It's the latest fashion in the Law Schools. These days, Grigori Romanovich, we mustn't just look at the facts, we must look at the motives behind the facts.'

'It's getting a bit deep for me, sir.'

'Me, too. If a dog bites a man, why ask for its motive?'

'Why, indeed, Your Excellency?' said Novikov, guffawing again.

'Not only motives,' said Dmitri, 'but circumstances.'

It was coming to him now. Not just in what Stenka had said, but in what the women at the tannery had said.

'Ah, circumstances!' said Peter Ivanovich.

'What circumstances are there, then, Dmitri Alexandrovich?' said Novikov, mock innocently. 'Finding out how it is that someone can't read someone else's writing?'

He gave Peter Ivanovich a wink. The Presiding Judge responded with a thin little smile.

'Finding out who was actually put on the convoy,' said Dmitri. He turned to Stenka. 'A real Russian beauty, you said?'

'That's right, Your Honour.'

'Fair?'

'As straw in summer.'

'A Tatar?'

'Tatar?'

'Marfa Nikolaevna was Tatar.'

'This girl was no Tatar,' said Stenka uneasily.

'What are you saying?' said Peter Ivanovich sharply.

'Not saying; wondering,' said Dmitri. 'Whether the right woman was put on the cart.'

Whereas the woman put on the cart had been fair, almost silvery blonde in the characteristically North Russian way, Marfa Nikolaevna, they eventually established, was dark. It took them some time because although she had been tried in the Court House, she had not been tried in a regular court. As a political prisoner, she had appeared before a Special Tribunal of the Ministry of the Interior. The Ministry held its Tribunals in the same building as the ordinary Law Courts, but this was purely for convenience and the two administrations were quite separate. Peter Ivanovich could not, then, go directly to the Clerk of the Courts as he would otherwise have done, nor could he have an informal word with the lawyers involved since, despite the reforms of the eighties, out in the provinces political prisoners were not legally represented. Peter Ivanovich certainly knew the officer who had presided over the Tribunal that day – they met socially – but as a matter of protocol they never discussed each other's affairs. Judges in Russia, following the assassination of Tsar Alexander, had learned discretion.

It was with a certain diffidence, therefore, that Peter Ivanovich inquired about Marfa Nikolaevna.

'All I need to know about is her looks,' he said to Porfiri Porfirovich, the officer who had chaired the Tribunal on the day that Marfa Nikolaevna had been sentenced.

'Her looks?' said Porfiri Porfirovich incredulously.

'Yes. Whether, for instance, she is fair or dark?'

'Dark,' said Porfiri. 'But – '

'A real Russian beauty?'

'Hardly. A Tatar.'

'I was afraid so,' said Peter Ivanovich, sighing heavily.

'What *is* this?' said Porfiri.

'A possible case of…' Peter Ivanovich didn't know what it was a possible case of. 'Mistaken identity,' he tried.

Porfiri Porfirovich's eyebrows shot up.

'On our part,' said Peter Ivanovich hastily. 'Or, at least, not on our part; possibly on the part of the Convoy Administration.'

But the Convoy Administration, too, came under the Ministry of the Interior and Porfiri Porfirovich's eyebrows stayed raised.

'Or, most likely of all,' said Peter Ivanovich, adapting with the speed born of long years in the Russian judicial system, 'it simply fell between stools.'

'*What* fell between stools?'

'This – this confusion.'

'I can see that *you* are confused, Peter Ivanovich,' said Porfiri sharply; 'but over what?'

Peter Ivanovich was forced to tell him all.

'The trouble is,' he concluded, 'the Marfa Nikolaevna who was sentenced was dark, while the Marfa Nikolaevna who got on to the cart was fair. And definitely not a Tatar.'

'Simple,' said Porfiri Porfirovich. 'The sergeant gave him the wrong name.'

'Yes,' said Peter Ivanovich unhappily, 'that's what we thought. At first. But then we checked. There were only five women that day in the political cart and the soldier, Stenka, remembers them all. None of them were Tatar. Three of them were in their fifties, whereas this Shumin woman was – '

'In her thirties.'

'Exactly. And of the other two, one was nursing a baby and the other was, well, blonde in the Russian style. So where is the real Marfa Nikolaevna?'

'In the prison. She must have been put in the wrong cart.'

'We have been to the prison. We have checked all the prisoners who were readmitted that day. None of them,' said Peter Ivanovich, 'is Marfa Nikolaevna.'

Porfiri Porfirovich frowned.

'Are you sure? Quite sure? Who did the checking? You can't rely on the prison officers.'

'Novikov,' said Peter Ivanovich. 'He went over there and checked them personally.'

'Novikov's a fool,' said Porfiri dismissively.

'I sent young Kameron with him. You know, the new Examining Magistrate. You can say a lot about young Kameron, I know,' said Peter Ivanovich quickly, as Porfiri opened his mouth, 'but what you can't say is that he isn't bright.'

'Well, if you're sure,' said Porfiri. 'That means she must have been in our cart. The soldier's simply got it wrong.'

'I hope so. But, um, you wouldn't care to check, would you, Porfiri Porfirovich? Because the only alternative, if she's not in the prison and she's not with the convoy, is that – '

'She's escaped. *Escaped*?'

Porfiri sprang to his feet.

'*Escaped*?'

Peter Ivanovich nodded unhappily.

'From the Court House at Kursk?'

Peter Ivanovich nodded even more unhappily.

'Outrageous!'

'And improbable,' said Peter Ivanovich swiftly. 'Quite improbable! There will be some other explanation, I am sure. But – you will check, Porfiri Porfirovich?'

Porfiri pulled a writing pad towards him.

'I'll check, all right!' he said. 'And if – ' He swore terribly. 'The trouble is,' he said, 'that God knows where they have got to by now. Things have speeded up, Peter Ivanovich, in the last year or two, now that we can use the train. We get them to Moscow and after that it's train all the way to Perm. How many days is it since the cart left? We might just do it.'

He picked up the bell on his desk and rang it vigorously.

'We're going to have to get on with this,' he said. 'No hanging around. If something has gone wrong – My God! Escaped! From the Court House at Kursk! This is terrible!'

'It's even worse,' said Peter Ivanovich gloomily. 'Because if she's not gone, someone else has. And I have a nasty feeling that ...'

He told Porfiri Porfirovich about Anna Semeonova.

'You damned fool!' shouted Porfiri. 'You've sent the wrong woman to Siberia!'

Which was hardly fair, Peter Ivanovich told himself as he walked back to his office, since if anyone had sent anyone to Siberia it was clearly Porfiri Porfirovich. He had an uneasy feeling, though, that when blame was finally attached, it would not be to the Ministry of the Interior. Meanwhile, there was the girl herself to be considered: Anna Semeonova, that was, not this wretched Shumin woman, who, from what Dmitri had said, seemed to have been asking for trouble anyway. The more Peter Ivanovich thought about the matter, the more convinced he became that Dmitri was right. If Marfa Nikolaevna had not been dispatched to Siberia, then somebody else had; and from the soldier's description – young, fair, 'a real Russian beauty' – it sounded very much as if it was Anna Semeonova. If so, goodness knows what was happening to her now. How she, a young girl of a sheltered, respectable family, would respond it was frightful to think. How her father, a man who had powerful friends, would respond, Peter Ivanovich had all too good an idea.

Among the other depressing things jostling in his mind as he walked back to his office was the prospect of having to tell Semeonov what had happened to his daughter. How on earth did you do a thing like that? 'Oh, by the way, Semeonov, about your daughter: we've worked out what must have happened. A silly mistake! Frightfully sorry, old man, but we've sent her to

Siberia!' The sheer idea was enough to start Peter Ivanovich thinking desperately about his pension. No one who had climbed as far up the ladder as he had done could be without influential friends. Peter Ivanovich now began hastily to review them, wondering which of them it would be best to turn to in the present emergency.

But wasn't he being premature? Wasn't it too early to tell the Semeonovs anything just yet? After all, he still wasn't sure. Why not wait until he was sure? To do otherwise might be merely to worry the parents unnecessarily. All might yet be well. It might all be just a silly mistake.

Not that mistake; a different one. Please God, prayed Peter Ivanovich, with a fervency hitherto unsuspected in him, let it all be a mistake!

And someone else's, he added.

But how on earth had it all happened? How could the girl have got herself into this situation? She must have been standing in the yard and one of the guards had naturally thought –

She would have protested, of course, but –

The fact was, she ought not to have been in the yard at all. He had said that all along. It wasn't a fit place for a decent young girl. Everyone knew that. No one, surely, needed telling? If you went there and got involved in something unpleasant, you had only yourself to blame. Although, of course, in this case ...

His thoughts were just coming round to Dmitri when he turned the corner and saw the conceited young puppy standing at the door of his room.

'I've had a thought,' said Dmitri unceremoniously.

Peter Ivanovich was just about to ask that he be spared when he remembered that it was Dmitri, after all, who had hit on the possibility that the wrong woman had been transported.

'Come in,' he said, with ill grace. His head was beginning to throb painfully. 'What was your thought?' he asked, forcing himself to make an effort.

'It's about the girl,' said Dmitri. 'Not Anna Semeonova, the other one.'

'Yes?'

Surely the man could see that his head was splitting?

'If what we're supposing is correct,' said Dmitri, 'then we know where Anna Semeonova is. But where is Marfa Nikolaevna?'

'Somewhere else in the convoy.'

'But surely not. First, because there was only one convoy cart for women that day and we've checked the people in it and none of them was her. Second, because if she was there, she would be under somebody else's name and there would be a person left over.'

Peter Ivanovich groaned and pressed his hand to his head.

'A migraine,' he said. 'Never mind; continue.'

Dmitri had not the slightest intention of minding. He continued:

'Since nobody was left over, however, someone must have removed themselves, literally, from the equation. As Anna Semeonova came *into* the yard, someone else must have gone *out*.'

'Yes, yes. Quite so,' murmured Peter Ivanovich. Had the man no feeling?

'Marfa Nikolaevna, of course.'

'Of course. Of course?' said Peter Ivanovich, waking up.

'And I think I know', said Dmitri triumphantly, 'where she went.'

'You do?'

'Yes. Straight out of the front door.'

'Oh, come!' said Peter Ivanovich. 'We checked with the porters, remember? And they swore – '

'That Anna Semeonova had not gone out. Anna Semeonova,' said Dmitri with emphasis; 'not Marfa Nikolaevna.'

'Well – '

'And they *did*, in fact, remember that another woman had left the building. A Tatar.'

Peter Ivanovich sat stunned.

'You mean …?'

'That Marfa Nikolaevna walked out of the front door, a free woman; while Anna Semeonova left from the back door – in a prison cart!'

'Impossible!' said Novikov. 'Prisoners are under guard all the time. From the moment they leave the dock to the moment they are put on the cart. And then afterwards all the time until they're either back in the prison or with the convoy. This Marfa Nikolaevna couldn't just walk out. Ridiculous!'

'She was seen by the porters.'

'They made a mistake.'

'Another one?' said Peter Ivanovich wearily. He was beginning to feel past caring. 'There do seem to be a lot of them about.'

'With all due respect, Peter Ivanovich, too much weight must not be placed on a single glimpse!'

'We're placing quite a lot of weight on Stenka's single glimpse,' said Dmitri.

'That was not a glimpse,' retorted the Chief of Police. 'That was a studied examination.'

'No doubt,' said Peter Ivanovich, 'the soldiers have nothing better to do than examine the female prisoners.'

'At least it means that they're watching them, Your Excellency,' said Novikov, beginning to perspire. 'So it makes it even more unlikely that one of them would have just … just walked off.'

'They're under guard all the time, are they?' asked Dmitri.

'From the moment they leave the dock.'

'Yes, yes, I've got that. But *all* the time? What happens if they want to have a pee?'

'How the hell do I know?' said Novikov, patience snapping. He pulled himself together and looked at Peter Ivanovich. 'Your Excellency, that is not a question one gentleman should ask of another!'

'Oh, shut up!' said Peter Ivanovich, placing his pounding head between his hands.

'Well, if you don't know, who would know?' demanded Dmitri.

'The soldiers in the yard, I suppose.'

'Well, let's go and ask them.'

'Your Excellency – ' Novikov appealed to the Presiding Judge.

'Oh, go and ask them!'

It couldn't get worse. He could imagine what people would say. His colleagues: 'And then he sent the Chief of Police to find out how the women peed! Well, really!' But Peter Ivanovich was past caring.

'Go on!'

There were some soldiers in the yard. While the courts were in session and until the prisoners started coming back down again they had nothing to do. They were standing around smoking.

Dmitri went up to them.

'What happens when the prisoners want to relieve themselves?'

'Relieve?'

'Pee.'

The soldiers looked puzzled.

'They get on with it.'

'Where?'

'Here.'

'In the yard?'

'Yes.'

'Where they stand?'

'More or less.'

'The women too?'

The soldiers looked at each other.

'You might let them go to one side,' they conceded.

'Out of sight?'

'Well, I wouldn't say that. Just – a bit away. Over against the wall.'

'Yes, over against the wall.'

'You heard that?' said Novikov. 'Not out of sight.'

'Suppose they were over against the wall and something happened to distract you, another party of prisoners arrived, say: would it be possible for them to slip away?'

'Where would they slip?'

'Through the door,' said Dmitri. 'That door there, say,' pointing at the door to which he and Anna Semeonova had come that ill-fated day.

'Well, it's possible, I suppose, but – '

'It's impossible, Dmitri Alexandrovich, absolutely impossible!' said Novikov firmly. 'Remember the situation that day: very few women prisoners. They'd have been under the guard's eye all the time. Now I know what you think of young Stenka. He said what he shouldn't have done and perhaps he did what he shouldn't have done; but the one thing you can't say is that he wasn't looking at them!'

'He was looking at Anna Semeonova,' said Dmitri, 'and while he was looking at her, Marfa Nikolaevna was sloping off.'

Porfiri Porfirovich listened in silence. When the Presiding Judge had finished, he paused for a moment and then said:

'So what you've done is to let a noted woman terrorist walk free and an innocent young girl be deported to Siberia?'

'I wouldn't put it quite like that,' said Peter Ivanovich.

'Noted woman terrorist?' said Dmitri.

'If she wasn't one already,' said Porfiri Porfirovich, 'she's probably become one by now!'

'It's not her, with all respect, that I'm worried about,' said Peter Ivanovich. 'It's Anna Semeonova.'

'A sensitive young girl,' said Porfiri, 'cast among some of the most hardened and brutalized people imaginable!'

Peter Ivanovich blenched.

'Don't, Porfiri Porfirovich,' he muttered.

'I don't see how you can hope to escape from this with impunity, Peter Ivanovich,' continued Porfiri Porfirovich pitilessly.

51

'Heaven knows what will have happened to her by the time we find her. Even if she comes back, she'll be a changed woman.'

'*Even* if?'

'A sensitive girl. Who knows what torments – '

'You think she really could …?'

Peter Ivanovich caught his breath.

'I think she'd better be found as soon as possible.'

'Well, yes. You're doing what you can, of course …'

His voice tailed away.

'It's a real pig's ear,' said Porfiri Porfirovich. 'I've sent messages. But you know our bureaucracy, Peter Ivanovich. Will they get through? If they do, will anybody do anything? It's an awkward business, you see, and people will want to steer clear of it. It's the kind of thing they'll pass from one desk to another. And meanwhile …'

'We must do something,' said Peter Ivanovich. 'You said yourself, we must do something!'

'I'd send someone,' said Porfiri. 'That's the best way. When you're actually there, they can't fob you off. At least, not if you've got authority.'

'You don't think – you don't think,' said Peter Ivanovich timidly, 'that you could go yourself, Porfiri Porfirovich?'

'No,' said Porfiri, 'I don't. I've got a job to do here. Made even more difficult by the incompetence of the local administration.'

'Then who?'

'It ought to be someone who could identify the girl. Properly, I mean. We've had enough of that sort of mistake.'

His eyes turned to Dmitri.

4

'So you agreed?' said Sonya, eyes shining.

'I said I would think about it.'

They were in Igor Stepanovich's sitting room. There was a row of glasses on the table and the vodka had already been started. Igor had intended the get-together as a gesture of solidarity – he had felt that Dmitri would need support after talking to Porfiri Porfirovich – but it had somehow turned into a celebration. They were all there, the usual circle, plus Sonya and Vera Samsonova.

'But you will, won't you?' said Sonya.

'At the time, I thought I would. Now I am not so sure.'

'Why?' asked Vera.

'Because it would be so unpleasant.'

'But you wouldn't mind, would you?' said Sonya.

'I think I certainly would.'

'Yes, but you would bear it for the sake of Anna Semeonova!' declared Sonya.

Dmitri's attachment to Anna Semeonova, however, had dwindled.

'But why *should* I bear it? I hardly know the girl.'

'Dmitri!'

'Well, it's true, isn't it?'

'She called to you for help!' said Sonya reproachfully.

'It was only help in finding the back yard!'

'Oh, no, Dmitri, it was a cry from the heart!' said Sonya confidently.

The girl had clearly been reading too many novels. Dmitri had always known it would be a mistake if they admitted women to their circle.

But it wasn't just the women.

'You can't abandon her now!' said Sonya's brother, Pavel.

'I am *not* abandoning her. She has never been mine to abandon. I met her once, casually, in the Court House. That is all!'

'It is your duty!' said Igor Stepanovich sternly.

'Duty! How can it be?'

'Your duty as a lawyer to your client.'

'She's not my client. I just met her casually in the corridor.'

'She asked you for advice and you gave it. I would say that constitutes acceptance of her as a client. De facto, if not de jure.'

Igor Stepanovich had once studied law. Briefly.

'De facto?' said Dmitri, outraged. 'What sort of nonsense is that?'

'What do these legal quibbles matter, anyway,' said Sonya passionately, 'when there is a prior claim of the heart?'

'Heart? Whose heart?'

'Not yours,' shot Vera Samsonova. 'Not yours, because you haven't one!'

'Oh, not got one, haven't I?' cried Dmitri furiously. 'Well, let me tell you, no one would have even thought of going to Siberia if it hadn't been for me!'

'Oh, you're very good at your job, Dmitri,' said Vera Samsonova spitefully. 'No one doubts that. It's just that we wonder if there is anything else in you apart from your job.'

Dmitri banged his fist on the table and made the glasses jump.

'You think it's part of my job? To go to Siberia?'

'It's your moral duty, man!' shouted Igor Stepanovich, crashing his fist, too, upon the table. 'As one human being to another!'

'That won't weigh with Dmitri!' cried Vera Samsonova. 'All he thinks about is his precious career.'

'Do you think it's in the interest of my career *not* to go to Siberia? Quite the reverse, I can tell you. Quite the reverse!'

'I'm sure you've calculated it very carefully,' said Vera Samsonova nastily.

'Oh, Dmitri, how could you?' cried Sonya. 'To think of your career when a woman's life is at stake!'

She began to cry noisily.

'You brute!' shouted Igor Stepanovich. 'All you think about is yourself!'

'You have no heart!' cried Vera Samsonova, beginning to weep too. 'You have no heart!'

'I have a heart!' shouted Dmitri. Why this should suddenly be so important to him was not clear.

'Show it then!' cried Sonya. 'Take suffering upon you!'

'Suffering?' said Dmitri, far, but not quite, gone.

'For the sake of mankind!' shouted Igor Stepanovich.

'And womankind,' sobbed Vera Samsonova.

'I will!' shouted Dmitri.

Train to Moscow, bearable: train on to Nizhni Novgorod tedious. The countryside was flat and featureless, the passengers on the train pretty featureless, too. There wasn't a pretty woman among them, nor an interesting man. Dmitri retired to his book. It was a novel. Dmitri didn't believe in reading official papers.

The train stopped at Nizhni Novgorod; or, rather, the track ran out. After this it was boat. Dmitri had never been on a boat, but he could guess what it was like. Everyone crowded together and no privacy. And so slow! He decided to avoid it if he could, and went straight to the police station.

Well, not quite, or, at least, not entirely intentionally. In fact, the police came to him.

It happened like this. When Dmitri got off the train he was amazed. He was amazed, first, because there weren't any people. There were the buildings, quite substantial ones, some of clay, brick, too; there were the boulevards, wide and shaded by not yet leafy birches and poplars; there were the hotels, the theatres, the enormous cathedral of Alexander Nevski, even a Bourse – a stock exchange, for God's sake! And there were the markets.

But there was no one in them. Grass and weeds grew in the middle of the empty streets. The shops were all shut. The doors and windows of the houses were all shut. There wasn't a vehicle in sight. Vehicle? There wasn't even a pedestrian. He had come into a ghost town.

At last he saw someone, a peasant carrying a load of wood.

'What the hell's going on?' said Dmitri. 'Where is everyone?'

The peasant, glad of the excuse, put his load down.

'*Nothing's* going on,' he said. 'That's the point. It doesn't go on till the summer.'

Gradually, Dmitri worked it out. Nizhni Novgorod was a fair city and this side of the river was where the fair was, but it didn't open until May. When it did, the place would be full. Five hundred thousand traders would flock into the city. Until then, though, the buildings stayed empty.

But if there were no people, there were hundreds of boats. They lined the banks of the Volga for six miles on both sides. That was the second thing that amazed Dmitri. It was a boat world. There mightn't be vehicles on the streets but there were plenty of boats on the river, of all shapes and sizes and sorts, some sail, some rowing, some – the larger ones – steam.

A thought struck Dmitri. He had been intending to go to the police station, but why go there? If they were anything like the police in Kursk, they wouldn't know anything. The people who would know would be the boatmen. This was where the prisoners were trans-shipped from rail to boat, and the boatmen would know how frequently and from where the prison boats left. He could go straight there. If he went to the police station, the chances were that it would take him quite a long time to work his way through their bureaucracy, and by that time Anna Semeonova might have departed.

The boatmen obliged. The convict barges, they said, left from a point some two miles down the river. There was a sort of cantonment in which the prisoners were kept. It was on this side of the river because that's where the train terminal was and they didn't want to go to the trouble of ferrying them to the other bank.

'Get them on board once and that's it!' they said.

Dmitri thanked his stars that the idea had occurred to him before he'd gone to all the trouble of crossing to the other side and negotiating with all the Novikovs the police station probably contained. He looked around for a droshky. Of course, there wasn't one, so he had to make his way on foot. In summer, no doubt, it would have been delightful; the Volga, blue and brimming with boats on one side, the bazaars with all their Tatar traders on the other. This early in the year it was bloody cold.

The cantonment was easy to pick out. It consisted of a number of long wooden buildings surrounded by a high wooden palisade. Finding himself confronted by the palisade, Dmitri began to walk round it in search of a gate.

He had nearly got to the gate when two men in uniform came up to him.

'What are you doing?' they said.

'Trying to find my way in,' said Dmitri.

'Are you sure it's not trying to help someone to find their way out?' they said suspiciously.

'It would be a public service,' granted Dmitri, 'which I certainly hope at some time to perform. Meanwhile, I would like to talk to someone responsible. Assuming that there *is* someone responsible in a place like this.'

It was then that they arrested him. To Dmitri's chagrin, they took him not into the cantonment but to the police station on the other side of the river, where it was some time before he found intelligent life at all and considerably longer before, even with the aid of his authorizations, he was able to persuade them of the genuineness of his mission and to transport him back to the cantonment. Where he discovered that the barges containing the Kursk consignment had just left.

There was nothing else for it; to Perm he would have to go. It would take weeks. Perm, as far as Dmitri was concerned, was on the edge of the known world. Go further and you would fall off – into a region where there were great blank spaces on the map with 'Here be anthropophagi' written across them: Siberia, in fact.

Could he be spared for so long? All too easily, he felt. They were probably glad to get rid of him. What of the cases he would miss? Well, what of them? There were too many of the 'she put a spell on my cow' sort. No one was going to make a name for himself by working on that sort of thing. No, he would probably do far better for himself by finding Anna Semeonova and bringing her back to the relieved arms of her parents. Old Semeonov was supposed to have influence. What was the name of that prince he was always talking about? Dolgorukov? 'Ah, Prince, can I introduce the young man who rescued my daughter?' 'Kameron? An unusual name, that. Scottish? Well, it's one that I shall certainly remember.'

Dmitri chided himself. That sort of thing was for Peter Ivanovich. He would have nothing to do with it. He would carve his way upwards by legal brilliance alone. He would rescue Anna Semeonova purely because it was his duty.

In the cause of duty he was prepared to suffer, even to the extent of enduring a tedious journey by boat. Setting himself sternly, he went down to the river and found a Kamenki Brothers steamer going in the right direction.

It was about a thousand miles from Nizhni Novgorod to Perm by river, first down the Volga and then up to the Kama and fortunately the weather was mild enough for him to spend the whole time outside, up on the hurricane deck, away from the throng of muzhiks below, smoking, smelling, chattering and, yes, he had guessed it would come to that, singing. Put a Russian on the river and he would at once start singing about Mother Volga.

There were never more than a few people on the hurricane deck since it was reserved for gentlemen, a term, however, used fairly loosely on the river. Most of them stayed on for only a short distance. Only two other men, beside Dmitri, were going the whole way. One of these was an elderly merchant, wrapped heavily in furs and apparently hibernating since he said nothing at all for the whole of the first day. The other was a young railway engineer over-eager to engage Dmitri in conversation.

'Ah!' he said ecstatically, breathing in heavily and taking in the scene with a wide sweep of his hand. 'The real Russia!'

'Is it?' said Dmitri discouragingly.

He distrusted people who talked about 'the real Russia'. All too often they were people of a certain sort, people who identified the real Russia with a very unreal Old Russia, in which peculiar spiritual insight was somehow to be found in simpletons and wisdom was lodged in the *startsi*, or elders, of the local peasant community. Dmitri did not believe that wisdom was lodged in anybody old and thought that Holy Fools were more likely to be fools than holy. He was a staunch modernizer and believed that Russia's problems would be better solved by turning towards the west, than looking inwards to the past. And he was surprised that this young man, an engineer and therefore, according to Vera Samsonova at least, more likely to be in tune with the modern spirit, did not think so too.

'Do you know how much trade goes down this river?' said the engineer.

'Certainly not!' said Dmitri coldly.

'Five million tons. Five million tons!'

'Really?'

'Seven hundred boats carrying grain alone!'

He was probably not, then, an 'Old Russia' man; he might even be a modernizer. All the same, Dmitri did not feel inclined to forgive him. He would not forgive anyone who used statistics.

He turned away from the engineer and addressed himself, with apparently significant concentration, to the landscape; which proved to be much like landscape. The left bank was totally uninteresting, flat and wooded. The right bank was at least varied. The land rose up abruptly from the water's edge to a height of about 500 feet and was broken by promontories which divided the river into a series of long, still reaches, rather like lakes. Here and there on the promontories were white-walled churches with silver domes, surrounded by little villages of unpainted wooden houses, with elaborately carved and decorated gables. Occasionally, the steamer would run close in to the bank and then sometimes they would see muzhiks lying about on the grass (idle sods; they were the real Russia, all right) in red shirts and black velvet trousers. Sometimes, too, there were peasant girls who would run down to the river waving their handkerchiefs. It was all very picturesque. Dmitri, however, was opposed to the picturesque. He objected to anything that conjured out the emotionally facile in you.

He stayed morosely peering out at the bank until it became dark. Then, suddenly, the merchant roused himself and summoned a samovar from below and the fragrance of the tea was so inviting that Dmitri was lured back to sociability. He exchanged grunts with the merchant and even asked the engineer what (on earth) he was going to do in Perm.

'Oh, I'm working on the railway,' said the young man, pleased to tell him.

'Railway?' said Dmitri. 'Out here?'

'The Ural Mountain Railway,' said the engineer, shocked. 'It goes from Perm to Ekaterinburg.'

'Why?' asked Dmitri.

'Well, the mines, of course ...' His voice trailed away. He was clearly wondering whether Dmitri was having him on. 'And the prisoners,' he added, deciding that he wasn't. 'At the moment we're working on an extension to Tiumen. It's the big forwarding place for all the convicts.'

'Amazing!' said Dmitri.

'Well, it is in a way. You wait till you see it! It's really modern, the most modern part of the whole Russian rail system.'

He prattled on about how well-ballasted the track-bed was, how excellent the rolling stock, how well-kept the track. No expense had been spared. Even the verst-posts were set in neatly fitted mosaics of coloured Ural stones.

Dmitri's mind, however, had gone off on its own track. He was thinking about Anna Semeonova and the system that had brought her here, the system which, improving all the time, now brought nearly twenty thousand prisoners to Siberia every year. Ancient, he thought, or modern? The Old Russia or the New?

At about five o'clock in the morning he was awakened by the persistent blowing of the steamer's whistle, followed by the stoppage of the engine, the jar of falling gang-planks and the confused trampling of feet above his head. Guessing that they had arrived at Kazan, he went on deck.

For a moment, when he looked at the bank, he felt that he had been hit by the aurora borealis. The houses, all wooden, of course, had been painted a variety of colours. Just behind the landing-stage was a chocolate-brown house with yellow window shutters and a green roof. Next to it was a lavender house with a shining tin roof; a crimson house with an emerald roof; a sky-blue house with a red roof; an orange house with an olive roof; a house painted bright green all over; and then a house which over three storeys exemplified the entire chromatic range.

Stunned, he was about to retreat when he realized that this wasn't Kazan at all but just the Kazan *pristan*, or landing-stage. The city itself was over to the right, a mass of towers, minarets and domes shimmering in the early morning sunlight. It took him by surprise. He had been expecting a European city, but this wasn't European, it was something more Eastern. He had a slightly uncomfortable feeling of foreignness.

It made him think, oddly, of law books. He tried to recall what he had read of the origins of Russian law. Was Russian law European or Eastern? Up till now he had always taken it for granted that it was European. But Russian law had its origins in decrees of the Tsar and had no existence apart from the sovereign. In this it was more Eastern than European.

An interesting point, thought Dmitri, but one of purely historical interest.

It took the steamer another four days to reach Perm, by which time Dmitri was thoroughly fed up. His original prejudices had been entirely confirmed: the boat *was* slow, the passengers *were* boring, and the Russia away from St Petersburg and Moscow, the 'real' Russia, as the Slavophils had it, completely without interest.

The real problem was that he had finished his book. After that, all he could do was either talk to the engineer, which even by the end of the first day had become a strain, or study the scenery. The trouble with that was that it was always the same: woods, woods and yet more woods, the occasional little wooden landing-stage, infrequent hamlets with their one-storey wooden houses. Everything wooden, thought Dmitri, jaundiced, including the people.

This was, perhaps, unfair, as he had not yet talked to any of them. But he did not need to. He could see at once that they did not read the latest periodicals.

Towards the end of the first day after Kazan they left the Volga and turned up the Kama, which was like the Volga only more so: more woods, fewer people, fewer white-walled, golden-domed monasteries. The banks were steeper and more rugged, the barges ruder and more primitive, crudely painted in the way of the houses at Kazan, all bright colours jumbled together, spiralling up the masts and spilling over the fronts (the bows, so the engineer informed him). The people, too, were brightly coloured, the men in blue, crimson, pink and violet shirts, the women in lemon-yellow gowns, scarlet aprons and short pink over-jackets. In civilized Russia traditional costume was reserved for feast-days and holidays. Here it seemed to be holidays all the time. It was with some relief that he saw Perm approaching.

Having learned from his experience at Nizhni Novgorod, this time he drove straight from the landing to the police headquarters. The Chief of Police looked at him suspiciously, and even more suspiciously when Dmitri told him his errand.

'Show me your passport,' he said.

'Passport?' said Dmitri.

'You need a passport to travel in Siberia,' said the Chief of Police.

'But this isn't Siberia!'

'You're going there, aren't you?'

'Not if I can help it,' said Dmitri.

'You need a passport.'

This was the kind of exchange that usually brought out the worst in Dmitri. Realizing, however, that it would only lead to further delay, and, perhaps, crucial delay as it had done in Nizhni Novgorod, he fought hard to keep his temper.

'I have, of course, the necessary authorizations,' he said, dumping them on the desk in front of the Chief of Police.

The Chief of Police took his time looking through them. Dmitri told himself to be charitable. Maybe the man just found it hard to read.

'Your authorizations are incorrect,' said the Chief of Police at last, looking up triumphantly.

'In what respect?' demanded Dmitri.

'Wrong line,' said the Chief of Police, pointing with his finger.

Dmitri, however, was not a lawyer for nothing.

'I don't think so,' he said. He pointed with his own finger. 'You need to refer back to the main clause. An entry is required in that space only if the condition in the main clause is unfulfilled. Since that is not the case here, as Sub-Clause Two makes clear, no entry is required.'

'The authorization is still invalid,' said the Chief of Police. He was, however, impressed. 'What did you say you were here for?'

'I'm trying to trace a prisoner, mistakenly included in the exile convoy – '

'Exile? Oh, in that case you've come to the wrong place. What you need is the Bureau for Exile Administration.'

'And where is that?'

'On the other side of town,' said the Chief of Police, smiling.

Dmitri managed to leave without saying a word; a not inconsiderable moral triumph in his case.

The Bureau was there but closed.

'When is it open?' he asked a passer-by.

'Oh, it's open,' the man assured him. 'It's just that Simeon likes his vodka.'

'Where is he?'

The man pointed to a nearby *traktir*.

Dmitri went inside. There were several men sitting at tables. 'Simeon?'

'I'm Simeon,' said one of them, still, fortunately, sober. Just.

Dmitri sat down opposite him.

'I'm trying to trace a prisoner, a woman, mistakenly deported – '

'You'll have to ask the police.'

'I have asked them. They sent me to you.'

'Ah, but they're the ones who really deal with it. You'll have to go back to them.'

Instead of hitting the ceiling, Dmitri, wisened by his experiences, considered.

'If I bought you a drink,' he said, 'would you give me some advice?'

'I might well.'

'I'm trying to trace a prisoner, a woman, mistakenly deported,' said Dmitri, the bottle between them.

'Where is she from?'

'Kursk.'

'That consignment went through yesterday.'

'I was told they stopped here for a bit. Isn't this a transshipment point?'

'It is. But things have speeded up, now that we've got the new railway. The train sits waiting in the siding. All we have to do is march them across.'

'So they've already gone?' said Dmitri slowly.

'That's right. Yesterday morning.'

Dmitri needed another vodka.

'You'll have to go to Ekaterinburg,' said Simeon, who needed another vodka too. 'You'll definitely catch up with them there. It's the end of the railway and it always takes them some time to sort them out before they go on.'

'Ekaterinburg!'

Perm had always been his worst case. Even Porfiri Porfirovich had not envisaged him going beyond.

'It's not far,' said Simeon encouragingly. 'Not now that we've got the railway.'

'How far?'

'A day. The train leaves at nine in the evening and gets to Ekaterinburg at eight the following evening.'

'Won't I need a passport?'

'A passport? Why?'

'Don't you need one in Siberia?'

'Ekaterinburg isn't in Siberia. It's still in Russia!'

How could he give up now? When it was only one more day?

'You're sure. They'll stop there?'

'Certain sure. They've got to get them on to wagons. You know what wagons are. They'll have to sort them out into the right groups, get them loaded ...'

Dmitri took another drink.

'I'll do it,' he said.

The railway was indeed splendid, although Dmitri did not find that out until the next morning, when he woke to find the train stationary at a place called Biser. Biser was almost at the summit of the Urals and above the mists and cloud which clung to the forests below. All around was the heavy smell of pinewood resin. For most of the morning the train was running through forest-clad hills, with lumber camps the only sign of human habitation, except that occasionally it passed placer mining camps where hundreds of men and women were at work washing auriferous gravel. It was almost agreeable.

Though not as agreeable as when they stopped for lunch. This was at a station called Nizhni Tagil, on the Asiatic slope of the mountains. The dining room into which all the passengers filed had a floor of polished oak, a high dado of dark-coloured wood of a sort which Dmitri did not recognize, walls covered with oak-green paper and a stucco cornice in relief. Down the centre of the room ran a long dining table, set with snowy napkins, high glass epergnes and crystal candelabra, and piled high with artistic pyramids of wine bottles. For every two chairs there was a waiter in tails, white tie and spotless shirt front.

'Very modern, yes?' said a voice beside Dmitri.

It was the engineer.

'Modern?' said Dmitri. That was not quite how he would have put it. Although he was not complaining, especially as Porfiri had said he would foot the bill.

'Only the best,' said the engineer proudly.

Slightly dazed, Dmitri sat down. Instantly, soup was brought, and not your cabbage soup, either, but bouillon.

'Yes, I see,' said Dmitri. 'But why?'

The engineer looked puzzled.

'Why the best? Here? Who's it for?'

'Passengers. Mining engineers. Company people.'

'I see. Well,' said Dmitri, 'I suppose you've to lay it on a bit to get them to come here at all.'

'Ekaterinburg is a very cultivated city,' said the engineer, injured. He pulled a newspaper out of his pocket and opened it on the table. 'You see?' he said. '"Meeting of the Ural Society of Friends of the Natural Sciences". Opera. Exhibitions. The latest geological findings.'

'But the news is a month out of date!' said Dmitri.

'Ah, well …'

The engineer looked uncomfortable. 'It's not our fault,' he said. 'The papers have to go back to Moscow.'

'*Moscow*?'

'For approval.'

'You mean they're censored?'

'Aren't all papers censored?'

'Yes,' said Dmitri, 'but … loosely.'

'The nearer you get to Siberia, the less loose it gets,' said the engineer. Ekaterinburg, however, when they reached it that evening, seemed a normal Russian city. It had the usual wide, unpaved streets, the usual square log houses with ornamental window casings and flatly pyramided tin roofs, the usual white-walled churches with coloured or gilded domes and the usual *gostini dvor*, or city bazaar. Unusually, though, there were white globes of electric light hanging here and there over the broad streets, which they certainly didn't have in Kursk.

'Very modern,' said Dmitri, pre-empting the engineer's strike, as they were driven to the hotel in the droshky.

Less modern, however, was the sight of the prison carts the next morning lumbering on to the parade ground in front of the army barracks. What was worse was that they were empty and returning not going.

'Yes,' said the man in the Bureau cheerfully, 'they'll be well on their way now.'

'But they can only have got here yesterday!'

'I know. But we're very efficient. The wagons are all waiting for them when they get off the train. Besides, it's only the sick who need wagons. The rest walk.'

'Walk?'

'Until the new rail extension is built. It will take them all the way to Tiumen. We can't wait for it, I can tell you. They won't need to go through here at all. We won't even see them.'

'If they set out yesterday,' said Dmitri, 'and they're walking, they can't have got very far. If I took a droshky, couldn't I overtake them?'

'Well, you could,' said the man doubtfully, 'but I don't think it will help you. You're going to have to talk to the Administration, and that's at Tiumen.'

Dmitri sighed.

'How long will it take me to get to Tiumen?'

'Set out now,' said the man, 'take the horse express, and this time the day after, you'll be in Tiumen. You're sure to catch up with her there.'

'I've heard that before,' said Dmitri.

'Ah,' said the man, 'but Tiumen is different.'

The Tiumen forwarding prison was a rectangular three-storey brick building, seventy-five feet in length by forty or fifty in width, covered with white stucco and roofed with painted tin. It was surrounded by a whitewashed brick wall twelve or fifteen feet in height. At each corner stood a black-and-white zigzag-barred sentry box; and along each face paced a sentry carrying a rifle and fixed bayonet. Against the wall, on the right-hand side of the gate, was a small building used as the prison office.

On the ground in front of the gate sat a row of women with baskets beside them. The baskets contained black rye bread, cold meat, boiled eggs, milk and fish pies for sale to the prisoners.

There were sentries at the gate, which was locked and barred. As Dmitri approached, one of them called through a porthole in the gate and a moment or two later a door within the gate opened and a corporal came out. He looked at Dmitri's papers and then waved him through into the yard. Dmitri stood there for a moment while the corporal went off to find someone more senior.

There were about two hundred prisoners in the yard, some sitting idly in groups on the ground, others walking to and fro. They were all dressed in the same grey featureless clothes: a shirt and trousers of homespun linen, a long overcoat with one or two diamond-shaped patches of black or yellow cloth sewn upon the back between the shoulders, and a round peakless bonnet-style cap.

It took Dmitri a moment or two to register the strange sound. The air was filled with a peculiar continuous clinking, as of innumerable bunches of keys. He suddenly realized that almost all the prisoners were in chains.

Dmitri was used to the prisoners in the yard of the Court House at Kursk. Some of them had been in chains too. It had never, however, struck him as this did. Perhaps it was seeing so many all together. Or perhaps it was that the prisoners he had seen at Kursk had all only recently been free men and still retained something of the air of freedom. Even in the Court House they had been individuals. Here, individuality had been stripped away; or, at least, hidden beneath the uniform greyness. What remained was not faces but chains.

Was this what the back yard at Kursk led to? Dmitri had never before quite seen it like that. The back yard was, well, back;

pushed back so that no one could see it, at the back of one's thoughts, something one knew existed, had to exist, but which one preferred not to face.

Here, at Tiumen, the back yard of the world, or of Russia, at any rate, one could not help but look. The back yard had come up front.

5

'The Kursk consignment? Shumin?' The prison official looked at his papers. 'Yes, she's here.'

He led Dmitri out into the yard.

'The women are in a separate prison.'

He took Dmitri through a small gate in the outer wall of the prison. Opposite them was a high stockade made of closely set and sharpened logs.

'The women are in there.'

Inside were several barrack-like huts, each about thirty or forty feet long and about twelve feet high. The official glanced at his list and went into one of these.

It consisted of a large single room. Down the centre of the room, and occupying about half its width, ran the sleeping bench – a wooden platform twelve feet wide and thirty feet long, supported at a height of about two feet from the floor by stout posts. Each half of this low platform sloped a little, roofwise, from the centre, so that when the prisoners slept on it in two closely packed rows, their heads in the middle were a few inches higher than their feet. There was no other furniture apart from a large tub for excrement. Nor were there any blankets or mattresses. The prisoners slept on the bare wood in their over-coats.

The room was full of women and children, many of them lying on the sleeping bench. They stood up as the prison official entered.

'Now, girls, how are you?'

'Pretty well, thank you, Your Honour,' they chorused. Some of them even curtsied. They were nearly all, or so it seemed to Dmitri at first glance, ordinary peasants.

'Shumin's the one I want. Is she here?'

Dmitri had been looking. There were a number of blonde women, some strikingly so, but he could not see Anna Semeonova.

No one came forward.

The official inspected his list.

'Come on,' he said. 'She's down on the list. Where is she?'

The women conferred.

'She's not here, Your Honour,' said one of them hesitantly.

'I can see that,' said the official impatiently. 'Where is she?'

They conferred again.

'She was here, Your Honour.'

'All right, all right. Where is she?'

Considerable hesitation.

'We don't know, Your Honour.'

'Come on,' said the official sternly. 'She must be here!'

The women looked at each other. No one said anything, however.

'She's not in the yard?' The official went to the door and looked out. 'Visiting, is she?'

The women shook their heads.

'Don't know? Well, we'll soon find out!'

He walked briskly into another of the barracks.

'Shumin?'

'There's no one of that name here, Your Honour.'

He tried the next one, and then the others; with, however, the same result. He returned, vexed, to the original barracks.

'You're messing me about,' he said. 'And I don't like it. Now, where is she hiding?'

The women looked at him blankly.

'She *must* be here!'

He looked under the platform. There was nowhere else in the room where anyone could hide.

He looked at Dmitri.

'Do you know her? Do you see her? Come on girls, line up! Let's make sure.'

The women lined up along the edge of the platform. The children had stopped chattering and huddled to their mothers. Dmitri walked along the line. But he was sure already.

The Governor listened. He was a short grey-haired man in his mid-fifties and had the air of a martinet.

'Well, she must be here,' he said, 'if it says so on the forms.'

'But, Nikolai Razumovich, I've checked!' said the official.

'Check again. Get them all out in the yard.'

Dmitri went with him. The women all filed out of the huts and lined up in the yard. There were so many of them that they filled the yard.

Dmitri walked up and down the rows. Many of the women wore headscarves. The official made them take them off.

Dmitri looked closely. Might she not have changed? And did he remember her that clearly? He had seen her only once and that for a short time. Once or twice he stopped. On each occasion the official asked the woman her name eagerly. The names were never Shumin.

The official sent guards in to search the barracks. They returned unsuccessful.

'I know what it is!' said the official suddenly. 'She'll be in with the others.'

He took Dmitri out of the stockade and into another one. There were three long huts, each crowded to overflowing, this time with women, children and men.

'Families,' said the official. 'The women have chosen to go with the men.'

'Chosen?' said Dmitri.

'Yes. When their husbands were exiled they decided to go with them. It's not so bad out there, you know. At least, not in some parts. You're not in actual prisons. You're in settlements.'

The air was foul, the children crying. It was exactly the same as the other huts he had seen. There were no partitions and there was the same long, common sleeping platform.

The official asked the same question as before and received the same answer. He made them line up and got Dmitri to inspect them; with, however, the same result.

'She couldn't be with the men,' said the official doubtfully.

All the same, they went back to the main prison and into the men's barracks.

'Now, you bastards, you haven't got any women in here, have you?'

'If only we had!'

He made them line up. Dmitri's inspection this time was cursory. In these hard coarse faces there was no trace of Anna Semeonova.

The official wasn't looking at the prisoners anyway. He was turning over the coats left lying on the platform.

'What are you looking for, then?'

'Women.'

There was a general guffaw.

'You'll be lucky!'

He searched the piles of coats, though, with surprising thoroughness and then looked carefully under the platform.

'Try the shit-tub!' someone advised.

Dmitri was glad to get out into the open air.

'Feeling bad?' said the official. 'You get used to it.'

He called some men from the kitchens and they sprayed Dmitri from heat to foot with dilute carbolic acid.

'Just a precaution,' said the official. 'We've had a bit of an epidemic here.'

'What of?'

'Typhus.'

The carbolic acid suddenly smelt fresh; almost agreeable.

'What happens if people die?' asked Dmitri.

'We bury them.'

'Anna Semeonova – Shumin, that is; could she have died?'

'Not if she's on the list.'

However, back in the office he checked the lists, both the sick lists and the death lists. Shumin wasn't on them.

'They don't usually die on the way out,' said the official. 'It's later.'

He pushed the papers away and sat thinking.

'There's the cells,' he said doubtfully.

He took Dmitri into the main building. It contained the Governor's quarters, the kitchen, the hospital and the workshops, together with a number of separate cells. The cells were about ten feet by fifteen and housed from a dozen to thirty prisoners. The prisoners were different from the ones he had seen in the barracks. They were in ordinary, not convict, clothes. The prison official took off his hat when he went into one of the cells.

'With politicals,' he said, 'you never know. They may get to be important.'

'Shumin is a political,' said Dmitri.

In one of the cells a man was reading a book. It was dark in the cell and he was standing by the window holding the book up to the light. As they went into the cell he closed the book and came towards them.

'Well, Kiril Maximovich,' he said to the prison official, 'what can I do for you?'

'Have you got a woman in here, Grigori Yusupovich?' said the official, half jokingly. They seemed on good terms.

'A woman?' The man seemed surprised. 'No, I don't think so,' he said.

'For heaven's sake, Grigori!' said another of the prisoners. 'Don't you know whether we've a woman here or not?'

Grigori, slightly bewildered, returned to his reading.

'No,' said the other prisoner.

'A prisoner can't just disappear,' said Dmitri. 'Not from a place like Tiumen.'

'Nor have they,' said the Governor smoothly. 'There must have been an error in the papers.'

'Are you going to tell the Convoy Administration that?'

'What other explanation can there be?'

'That you've lost her.'

The martinet lips went thin.

'I don't think that's very likely. I think it far more likely that she never was here.'

'The forms say she's here,' Dmitri pointed out.

'Clerical error,' said the martinet.

'We have checked.'

'Check again!'

Dmitri felt his choler rising.

'I think *you* should check again,' he managed, however, with surprising mildness.

'I don't think so,' said the Governor coldly. 'The error plainly does not lie here.'

Dmitri considered.

'In fact,' said the Governor, pressing home, 'I suggest, young man, that you return to – where was it you said you came from? Kursk? – Kursk, and pursue your inquiries there.'

'I probably will do so,' said Dmitri meekly, 'only I would like to be able, when I get there, to reassure Prince Dolgorukov – '

'Prince Dolgorukov?'

'A friend of the girl's family. As I was saying, I would like to be able to assure the Prince – '

This time all the women, in all the different parts of the prison, were being brought out for inspection. There were too many of them to line up in the yard of the women's prison so they were being brought out on to the road that separated the women's prison and the family prison from the men's prison. The gates of the men's prison were open for officials to pass to and fro, and a crowd of its inmates had gathered to observe the proceedings, held back by a row of guards.

Dmitri hovered uncertainly. He had spent the morning in the office with some officials checking the prisoner lists. Yes, it appeared, Shumin's name was in the general arrival list. No, it was not on any of the sick lists, nor, fortunately, on the list of the dead. The list of the transfers out? Some prisoners were transferred out most days, on their way to postings to towns and settlements and prisons in the more remote parts of Siberia.

'She wouldn't have been posted on as quickly as that,' the officials assured him.

Nevertheless, he checked the lists. No Shumin appeared; nor did anything – bearing in mind the misunderstanding that had arisen at Kursk over handwriting – that could conceivably have been taken for Shumin.

There had been a roll call when the prisoners arrived. Shumin's name was on that. It appeared, then, that she had definitely arrived; and that she had not departed.

The officials, though, hesitated.

The roll call on arrival, they said, was not, perhaps, as watertight as it might be. The prisoners had, after all, walked from Ekaterinburg. It had taken them several days, nearly a week, in fact, and on the way the convoy would have stretched out. The last stragglers would have arrived many hours after the first.

Not only that; the sick, the pregnant and those fortunate enough to cadge a lift would have come on the carts, which would have arrived before any of the walkers. The consignment would not, therefore, have arrived together. They would have been ticked off on the list when they did arrive, but the roll call was not, the official pointed out, a roll call in the true sense.

What was a roll call in the true sense? asked Dmitri. What they were having now: a parade at which everyone answered individually by name.

More and more women came out of the prisons and assembled in the road. It was taking ages. Some of the women had already been standing there for an hour. In fact, the guards did not insist on them standing. They were allowed to sit and many of them squatted down in the road.

Some of them appeared to be enjoying it. They waved to the male prisoners crowding at the gate. The men called back with enthusiasm. The crowd had grown bigger now. Almost all the men allowed in the yard had gone over to the gates. Some had climbed on to others' backs in order to be able to see better.

Dmitri paced up and down, miserably, in the space left behind them. Only a few men, too weak or too ill to stand, had not joined the spectators. They sat or lay with their backs against the wall of the prison building.

One of the men looked up at him as he passed.

'A beautiful day, is it not, Brother?'

It was not; but Dmitri, taken by surprise, muttered some response. The man must be simple. He had an open, innocent face and looked up at Dmitri trustingly.

'God hears our prayers,' he said.

That confirmed it. He was simple. You met them all over the place. More often in the country than in the town, but even in

78

Kursk Dmitri had occasionally come across them, standing vacantly in the street, brought coppers by the children or bowls of *kasha* by the women. There were lots of beggars in Russia but holy ones had a special standing. They were treated with clumsy tolerance and even given a certain respect. There were those who claimed that in compensation for their affliction they stood in a special relationship with God. This, to Dmitri, was superstition. In his view they were all cracked. As this one probably was.

One of the officials came hurrying towards him.

'We're about ready now,' he said.

Dmitri pushed his way through the crowd and out between the gates. The women were now standing, a dozen great lines of them, stretching right along the road in front of the main prison. The senior official began to take him up and down the lines.

It was a ridiculous operation. The further he got, the more convinced of that he became. If Anna Semeonova had been here, surely it would have emerged by now? Surely she would have spoken up? Or someone would – if only to save them from all this bother.

Several of the women were looking round. Men were going into the women's prison, first, guards and then orderlies carrying huge pails. The pails contained disinfectant. The prison authorities were seizing the chance of the mass evacuation to spray the barracks thoroughly. The guards were making sure that no women were left inside.

The end of the line was now in sight. What would he do when he got to the end and still hadn't found her? She had come, she had not left, she was still here, therefore. Only she wasn't.

The orderlies re-emerged with the pails. The guards came up and reported. Dmitri looked quickly over the women remaining. There were no blondes among them.

The senior officer looked at him inquiringly. He shook his head.

'They'll have to wait until the rooms have dried,' said the official.

The women sat down. A cold wind stirred their rags.

Dmitri went back through the prison gates. Just inside he saw the man who had spoken to him. A beautiful day? God hears our prayers? Not in Tiumen, he didn't.

The men prisoners, hungry for women, clung on at the gate. The orderlies, prisoners themselves, were returning with the pails. The pails were heavy wooden ones and one of the carriers stumbled under the weight. Some of the disinfectant splashed out and over one of the guards. The guard cursed and pushed the bucket away. For good measure he caught the orderly a blow with his rifle.

The butt slid excruciatingly down the man's shins. He doubled up in pain and stumbled. One of the guards on the other side pushed him back into line and he fell to his knees. The first guard lifted his rifle again.

'Here, none of that!' said a big prisoner standing in the front row of the crowd.

The guards turned on him immediately.

'What's it got to do with you?'

The butts began to go in.

There was a sudden commotion in the crowd and a man pushed through.

'No blows! No blows!' he cried.

He threw himself between the guards and the man they were pounding.

'Christ, another one!' said one of the guards.

They turned their attention to the newcomer.

'Stop it!' shouted Dmitri, and hurled himself forward.

The guards looked up in astonishment.

'I order you to stop it! This is in breach of the Regulations for the Treatment of Prisoners!'

'What do you know about it?' said one of the guards belligerently.

'I'm a lawyer.'

'Here, hold on a minute!' said another of the guards in alarm.

The new kind of lawyer was a relatively recent creation in Russia, a product of the Reforming Acts of the previous Tsar. Information travelled slowly in nineteenth-century Russia; not so slowly, however, for the guards not to have heard of them and know that they were bad news.

They stopped their beating. The fallen orderly picked himself up and ran off. The big prisoner shook himself, then caught hold of the man who had intervened and pushed him away into the crowd. As he disappeared behind the other prisoners, Dmitri saw his face. It was the man who had spoken to him.

Some time later he saw them again in the yard, talking together. He went over to them.

'You want to watch out, that's all,' the big man was saying. 'If you go round trying to get in the way every time you see a guard hitting someone, one of these days they'll really fix you.'

'No blows!' said the other man firmly. 'No blows!'

'What I'm saying is', said the big man, 'that there'll be plenty of blows and all coming your way if you don't look out!'

The littler man shook his head. The big man caught Dmitri's eye.

'That's the trouble,' he said. 'You can't reason with them. Not with Milk-Drinkers.'

'Milk-Drinkers?'

'He's a Milk-Drinker.'

Dmitri looked at the little man with interest. He had heard of Milk-Drinkers; just. They were one of the many sects that had sprung up in Russia after the Great Schism of the seventeenth century, which had split the Orthodox Church between those who wished to keep to the old rites and those who wanted to move with the Church hierarchy towards reform. The *Molokans* had wished to keep to the old ways. To which they had added their dietary principles and a few other ones.

'Do you take anything apart from milk?' he asked curiously.

The little man nodded.

'Bread,' he said. 'Fruit. Anything that grows.'

'But not meat?'

'No.'

'Why not?'

The little man puckered his face up.

'Blows,' he said.

'You've got to respect them,' said the big man, 'even if you don't go along with them.'

'What on earth is he doing here?' asked Dmitri.

'They won't pay taxes.'

'Why not?'

'Because the Government spends it on bad things,' said the Milk-Drinker.

'Like what?'

'Soldiers. Prisons.'

'Courts?' said Dmitri.

'Courts, too.'

'You've got to have courts. You can't do without law.'

'You don't need courts. Law is inside us.'

'Ah, yes. But suppose we disagree?'

'We're not going to disagree, though, are we?' said the Milk-Drinker. 'God's law is the same for all of us.'

'I'm afraid people do disagree,' said Dmitri, 'and that's why we have to have courts. Not only that; sometimes people know what the law is but break it all the same.'

'If they break it,' said the Milk-Drinker, 'that's because they're wrong in their hearts. And courts don't do anything about that.'

'Well …' said Dmitri.

'Courts mean blows,' said the Milk-Drinker. 'Oh, I know that's not how the Tsar intends it, but it's how it comes out. You don't make people good by adding blows to blows.'

'How do you make people good, then?' asked Dmitri.

'I don't know,' said the Milk-Drinker. 'I only know that you start by getting rid of the soldiers and prisons.'

'Didn't I tell you?' said the big man. 'There's no reasoning with them!'

The big man's name was Methodosius.

The Milk-Drinker nodded approvingly when he said this.

'It's a good name,' he said.

'It's the only thing good about me,' said the big man, and laughed.

The Milk-Drinker's name was Timofei. Once Dmitri had been talking to him for a little while the slight oddity of manner disappeared. He seemed in no way different from any of the other peasants who came into town on market days.

The same could not quite be said of Methodosius. On the face of it he was an ordinary peasant, too. He wore the same long smock-type shirt and baggy breeches, the same high boots beneath his convict coat, as they did – and this at a time when in the countryside dress was still an indicator of rank, as it had been in the old days, prescribed so by the Tsar. His face was as tanned as theirs were, perhaps even more so. Certainly he seemed a man who spent his days out of doors. And yet …

There was something different about him. Partly it was the way he wore his convict coat, open at the chest, as if he was determined not to conceal or confine the man beneath. He carried himself almost with bravado. No, perhaps bravado was not the word. Dmitri knew criminal bravado and this wasn't it. What it was, he wasn't quite sure. Independence, perhaps? He thought it best not to pry too closely.

They asked him about himself. He told them the truth, that he was a lawyer looking for a girl who had perhaps been transported by accident. They accepted what he said without comment. Perhaps, they, too, thought it best not to pry.

Dmitri could hardly expect his part in the incident at the gate to go unnoticed. He was, therefore, not surprised when the following morning he was summoned by the Governor.

'Sir,' said the Governor coldly, 'I must ask you not in future to interfere with my officers when they are carrying out their duties.'

'Their duties include beating up the prisoners?'

The thin lips tightened.

'This is not St Petersburg.'

'Evidently.'

The Governor looked at him coldly.

'You refuse my request?'

Dmitri thought quickly. If he refused, the Governor would almost certainly require him to leave.

'No,' he said. 'I do not refuse your request.'

The Governor allowed himself a little satisfied smile.

'Very well, then. In the short time that remains of your stay – '

'Short time?' said Dmitri.

The Governor looked at him in astonishment.

'You have surely satisfied yourself that the girl is not here?'

'She is signed in as having arrived.'

The Governor frowned.

'A clerical error, obviously. Which I shall have to take up.'

'You are saying that she never arrived?'

'That is quite certainly the case.'

'That, since her name appears on the convoy lists, she was somehow lost en route? Escaped, perhaps?'

'I think it far more likely that she was never dispatched.'

'More clerical error? At the other end, this time? There do,' said Dmitri, 'seem a lot of them around.'

The Governor glared at him.

'If there are clerical errors,' he said harshly, 'I think it more likely that you will find them at Kursk. To which I suggest you return. Speedily.'

Dmitri considered.

'No,' he said.

6

That was all very well but where had it got him? The Governor had acceded but with an ill grace. Dmitri had been allowed to stay on in the prison guest room while he prosecuted his inquiries. He soon learned, however, that in future he could expect little co-operation from the prison authorities. Officials who had previously been helpful now averted their faces embarrassedly. The guards, after what had happened at the gate, kept their distance. An invisible wall had gone up between him and everyone else.

Dmitri affected not to mind. The company was not so brilliant that he could not do without it, he told himself truculently; and would have told everyone else had the opportunity presented itself.

In the privacy of his room, however, he was forced to admit that his inquiries were now severely handicapped. Visits to barracks – and therefore conversation with their inmates – were now allowed only after a specific request and required the Governor's written permission. The prison records could be consulted, but only in the prison office and in the suddenly unhelpful presence of clerks. It was all very well antagonizing the Prison Administration but, without its help, how was he going to be able to do anything?

The big man seemed to have taken the little Milk-Drinker under his wing; and this morning it rather looked as if he needed to. Timofei's lip was cut and his cheek bruised.

'I told you!' Methodosius was expostulating. 'I told you, didn't I? I pleaded with you!'

'If it's the guards again – ' began Dmitri angrily.

'Not this time. It was just two blokes having a go at each other, and he has to step in. All right, they weren't very good and it wasn't worth watching, but if you don't like it, why don't you just leave them alone?'

'No blows!' said Timofei.

'Yes, all right, I know what you mean. It's the principle of the thing, yes, I know. But, look, if you stick your nose in, you're the one who's going to get the blows, and that doesn't help anyone, does it? I mean, it's sort of provoking them, isn't it? All that happens when you stick your nose in is that there are more blows. Now that's not right, is it? Adding to the blows that there are in the world? Why don't you just keep out of it!'

Timofei had to think this over.

'And another thing,' said Methodosius, 'cut down on the praying!'

'Oh, no,' said Timofei. 'I couldn't do that!'

'Well, cut down during the night, at least. Couldn't you shift some of it into the daytime? I mean, they're the same prayers, aren't they? What difference does it make if they come up during the daytime?'

'It's quieter at night. I can give my mind to it.'

'Now that's the very thing it isn't. It's not quieter at night. Not if you're praying. And why can't you pray just once or twice? Not all through the night. Out loud.'

'By praying out loud, I give witness.'

'Yes, but you see, it creates bad feeling. And you wouldn't want that, would you? Not if it leads to blows?'

'Well, no,' said Timofei, startled. 'Do you think it could do that?'

'Pretty sure of it,' said Methodosius. 'You want to have regard to the number of blows there are in the world and cut the praying down! At least at night.'

Over at the gate something was happening. Guards were running about.

'Is another convoy coming in?' asked Dmitri.

'No, it'll just be the stores wagon.'

The guards opened the gates and then, after a large cart had driven in, closed them again. The cart carried on to the kitchens. Prisoners came out to unload it.

'That's a soft number!' said Methodosius. 'Now why couldn't I get that instead of the buckets?'

'Buckets?' said Dmitri.

There were six men, two to each bucket. Methodosius saw that Dmitri was paired with him. They lined up in front of the guardroom with the empty buckets and then filed out through the gate, an armed guard behind them.

Dmitri had thought there might be problems, especially over the chains.

'Chains?' Methodosius had said. 'No shortage of chains in Tiumen!'

The bights had been stretched so that Dmitri was able to slip them on over his hands and his feet. The weight made him stagger. The convicts, much amused, made him practise. Experience, they had assured him, was the thing.

The party crossed the road. At the gate of the women's prison they stopped and the guard called through a spyhole. The gate swung open and they went into the yard. They stood there for a moment and then split up, two men going into each of the barracks. The guard meanwhile stood against the wall in a position from which he could see all three barracks.

'You've got two minutes,' he said.

'Two minutes? It'll take us more than that to unchip the ice!'

'I know what will take you more than two minutes, and it's not chipping the ice! Two minutes.'

'Oh, come on! Do us a favour!'

Methodosius produced a cigarette.

'All right,' said the guard, relenting. 'But that only earns you five minutes.'

Methodosius brought out another two.

'What have you got in mind?' said the guard. 'An orgy?'

Methodosius and Dmitri carried the pail inside.

'Hello, girls!' said Methodosius.

'Hello!' said one of the women. 'You're a new one, aren't you? We haven't seen you before!'

'You haven't seen my friend, either,' said Methodosius. 'He wants to talk to you. You go ahead,' he said to Dmitri. 'I've got my mind on other things.'

He strolled across to the other side of the barracks.

'I'm looking for a woman called Shumin,' said Dmitri.

'Someone else was looking for her.'

'It was me. Some of you said you knew her.'

'You?' The women, intrigued, gathered round.

'I haven't got long.'

'You're all right. Olga, go and talk to the guard!'

'Is it the nice one?'

'No. That'll make it easier.'

'I'm not going to talk to him for too long,' grumbled the woman, but went off obediently.

'Now, what is it you're after?'

'Shumin. Some of you said you'd seen her.'

'Yes. She was with us on the convoy.'

'Do you remember what she looked like?'

'Of course I remember!'

'Fair or dark?'

'Is this some sort of game? I can think of better ones. Fair.'

'Really fair?' What was the phrase? 'A real Russian beauty?'

'Polish, I would have said. And I didn't go much on her nose.'

'Don't be such a bitch, Irina. She was very pretty.'

'Is she your girlfriend?'

'No,' said Dmitri. 'I'm just trying to find – '

'I'll bet she is!'

'No, she's not. Look, just tell me, I haven't got long: where the hell is she?'

'Why are you trying to find her, then? If she's not your girl-friend?'

'I'm a lawyer – '

'Oh, yes? And they put lawyers on the shit-buckets these days, do they? Well, it's reasonable, I suppose.'

'It was the only way.'

'Well, I'm damned! Isn't that the Governor I see over there? On the end of a bucket? Well, it was the only way he could come and see us, I expect!'

In the end, Dmitri had to tell them everything. He didn't mind that, but they needed some convincing and it ate heavily into his few precious moments. They listened, however, with growing involvement.

'Poor Anya! I always knew there was something different about her!'

'She didn't say anything to you about any of this?'

'Not a word.'

'She kept herself to herself.'

'Oh, I wouldn't say that,' someone objected. 'She was always rather nice.'

'Well, you know what I mean. Nice, yes, but I always thought she came across as a bit of a lady.'

'Well, she *was* a lady!'

'Yes, but – '

'You got to know her on the convoy?'

'Oh, yes. And I don't think she was at all stand-offish, Lena, it was only when that man came along – '

'What man was this?'

'Oh, it was just someone pestering her. One of the politicals. She didn't know what to do about him – '

'That's what I meant, Raissa, when I said she was a bit of a lady. I mean, she didn't know how to handle him, did she? You or I would just have told him to bugger off, but she couldn't quite manage to do that, could she? He went on and on at her, and in the end all she could do was run away when he wasn't looking and move to some other part of the convoy – '

He could see Methodosius returning.

'She went to some other part of the convoy? And you didn't see her again after that? So you don't really know that she ever got to Tiumen.'

'She got to Tiumen, all right,' said one of the women. 'When we got in, I saw her.'

'You're sure of that?'

'Yes. She was standing by the gate. There was a little party to one side. I don't know what they were doing but she was one of them. I don't know where they went.'

'Could you find out?' he said urgently, as Methodosius came up.

'We'll try.'

'All right, girls?' said Methodosius. 'He's a nice boy, isn't he?'

'Quite nice,' said one of the women critically. 'You can bring him here again.'

They lifted the pail. Or, rather, tried to.

'Jesus, it's stuck.'

Methodosius knelt down and tried to shake the bucket free.

The guard put his head in at the door.

'Come on, come on! You've had time to work your way through the whole barracks!'

'It's iced on!'

'I'll bet what you've been busy with isn't iced on!'

The guard came across and hammered at the bottom of the pail with the butt of his rifle. As the pail jolted free, some of its contents spilled over the side. A sickening stench rose into the air.

'Come on, get that bloody thing outside!'

Dmitri bent and lifted. He felt the other side of the bucket go up easily as Methodosius took hold. The bucket tilted towards him and something spilled on to his hands.

The mail had come in and with it some letters for Dmitri.

'You may stay as long as you wish,' wrote Peter Ivanovich generously; adding, however, less satisfactorily: 'In fact, the longer, the better.'

'My dear Dmitri,' wrote Igor Stepanovich, 'we think of you all the time', which was gratifying. Less gratifying, and not just because of the typically inflated – and exhausted – metaphor, was the rest of the sentence: 'and if you do not return, your memory will forever burn like a bright coal in our hearts.'

Hardly more pleasing was the next paragraph:

'Things here have returned to normal. I ran into Novikov the other day and he told me that everyone was doing their best to put the unfortunate incident behind them. He said that it was all due to a minor clerical error which he, Novikov, had fortunately been able to detect, and that now the whole thing was being fast forgotten. He half hinted that it probably wouldn't have occurred anyway but for the presence of young, inexperienced lawyers. Do you think, Dmitri, he could have meant you? Oh, and Peter Ivanovich seems to have made it up with old Semeonov, which is, Peter Ivanovich says, what really matters …'

Dmitri threw the letter down in disgust. As he did so, he caught sight of a postscript scribbled on the back of the envelope: 'Sonya sends her love.'

Indeed, in another letter, she did; and much more besides. She sent her heartfelt admiration, her tenderest sympathy and her passionate devotion, in which latter she was joined by Larissa Philipovna, whom by chance she had met coming out of church the other day. She lived, she said, only for the day when he returned – that bit was all right, thought Dmitri – which, unfortunately, would probably be long deferred. She bravely faced the possibility that he might be much changed, worn, grey – grey? – but, surely, after such a profound spiritual experience, much Deepened.

Dmitri threw that letter aside, too, and turned to one from Vera Samsonova. It was very brief. In fact, she said, she would not have written at all, only she had come across something in a local newspaper that she thought might interest him. She enclosed the relevant extract.

It was a report of a demonstration that had occurred recently outside a local tannery. The demonstrators had apparently wished to draw public attention to the effect on the health of the locality – it was this that had attracted the attention of Samsonova – of the tannery's discharge of chemical wastes. The demonstrators had, naturally, been arrested and were awaiting trial. Inquiries had established that they came from outside the area, indeed, from another province altogether, but that their ringleader, who had, unfortunately, escaped arrest, was a local woman, one Marfa Shumin.

'Thinking?' said a voice suddenly.

Dmitri stopped, startled. It was a man sitting with his back against the wall. His face seemed vaguely familiar.

'Just brooding,' said Dmitri.

'I am thinking,' said the man. 'It's better.'

'Oh?' Dmitri fired up. No one was going to give *his* mental processes secondary status. 'And what', he asked condescendingly, 'are you thinking about?'

'Justinian's *Statutes*.'

'Really?' said Dmitri, taken aback.

'Yes. They're fresh in my mind, you see. I was editing them for publication. An academic edition,' said the man, with a shy smile. Dmitri recognized him now. He was the man he had seen reading a book in the cell.

'You're a lawyer?'

'I've never practised. I teach legal history in the Law Faculty at Kazan University.'

'I'm a lawyer,' said Dmitri.

'How interesting!' cried the man, sitting up. 'Then we'll have lots to talk about. What is your field?'

'Oh, general,' said Dmitri, 'general.'

'Probably wise. It's a mistake to specialize too early. It can become a blind alley. Look at me: I'm not yet thirty and my career's already at a dead end.'

'Surely not ... When you get back – '

'With Roman law as a subject? It's peripheral, my dear chap. In Russian universities anyway. And yet at one time, you know, it looked as if it could be central. That was after the Reforms, when it looked for a while as if Russia was going to adopt a modern European legal system. It's not going to happen, though, is it?'

'Not at once; but I'm sure it will happen. It's only a question of time.'

Belief in progress was an article of faith of the journals which Dmitri read back in Kursk.

'I wish I could be so sure. But when I look around me ... after all, we wouldn't be here, would we, if Russia had a legal system based, like those of other European countries, on Roman law.'

'Wouldn't we?'

It was only afterwards that he realized that the man had taken him for a prisoner too.

'Well, no. Roman law made a distinction between justice and administration. In Russia we have never made that distinction.

What the Tsar says is law. What his officials say on his behalf is law. There is no tradition of the law as an independent thing to which appeal can be made, not as there is in other European countries, which have all incorporated that distinction into their legal systems.'

Dmitri remembered now thinking something along these lines on the boat. At Kazan, hadn't it been? Perhaps he had read something published from the university and had associated the name with the idea.

'And so,' said his acquaintance, 'they can send us to Siberia by administrative decree, without us having a chance to challenge their charges in a court of law subject to proper judicial processes!'

'And all this comes about because our legal system is not based on Roman law?'

'That's right.'

'Hmm,' said Dmitri thoughtfully. Like all law students he had studied Roman law in his first year at university. As with most students, however, its significance had escaped him.

'Or, at least,' said the man, smiling, 'that's what I argue in my article.'

'Which article was this?'

'The one that got me exiled to Siberia.'

Thinking? He certainly was. About Marfa Shumin, for a start, who had clearly escaped exactly as he had supposed and who seemed at once to have resumed her political activity; and if demonstrating outside Lev Petrovich's tannery was a sample of it, then good luck to her! But also about Anna Semeonova, who seemed in some strange way to have become a surrogate for her.

An act of selection had clearly occurred at the Tiumen gate and the most likely basis for it was that she had been taken to be, like her alter ego, a 'political'. But if that was so, why had he not seen her in the cells where the other politicals had been put? True, in the dark he could have missed her. But then, why hadn't she spoken up? That was the question that kept troubling him. Why, if she had been deported by mistake, hadn't she simply declared herself? The only answer he could find was that she had been too frightened to. And that, he was beginning to feel, he could understand.

7

'But what are facts?' asked his learned friend, the prisoner from Kazan. Dmitri had not really meant to reopen discussions, but, seeing him sitting alone in the yard reading a book – a different book this time – he had been unable to resist.

Dmitri frowned. The facts of a case were what Examining Magistrates were called on to establish. Afterwards, the prosecution might proceed. The Magistrate, in the lower Courts like Kursk, that was, would lay the facts before the Court and the judges would make up their mind. On the basis of the facts laid before them. The defence might challenge here and there, especially the evidence of witnesses, but the case was based essentially on what the Examining Magistrate had been able to discover.

Take the present case, for instance: so far, the facts he had been able to discover about Anna Semeonova's disappearance were:

One, that Anna Semeonova was a remarkably pretty young woman. No, no, that was not a fact but a judgement. Leave that to the judges. The judges? Desiccated old sods like Peter Ivanovich? Certainly not! Dmitri was quite capable of judging for himself. Especially about pretty girls. Where was he?

One, then: a girl from one of the best families in Kursk had disappeared. That definitely was a fact.

Two, from the Court House in Kursk. Also a fact? Less definitely. That was where she had been last seen and Dmitri was the one who had seen her, so there was no doubt about *that* as a fact. But had she gone out of the building and *then* disappeared, or had she disappeared from the Court House itself? A terminological quibble, Dmitri decided. No, she had disappeared from the Court House, and –

Three, Dmitri reckoned to know how it had been done: she had taken the place of Marfa Shumin. Why or how, he was not quite sure. Especially why – if why there was and it was not all just a complete balls-up on the part of the Convoy Administration. Anyway, Shumin had walked free and Anna Semeonova had been transported to Siberia.

That was Fact Four. She had definitely arrived at Tiumen Prison. Definitely? Well, pretty definitely. Her name – or rather, Shumin's name – had been ticked off on the list and she had been seen by reliable witnesses.

But what the hell had happened then? That fact was missing.

'Somehow the facts are hard to ascertain,' he said.

'Well, of course,' said his learned friend from the University of Kazan, 'and that is because of their very nature.'

'Nature?' said Dmitri suspiciously, and looked again at the title of the book that his acquaintance was reading: *Metaphenomenology and the Law: a Hegelian Approach.*

'Yes. You think of facts as something out there that you can discover. The truth for you is objective.'

'Certainly,' said Dmitri.

'But suppose it is not? And the only thing that exists are different versions of the truth? What then are facts?'

'Just because people speak about them in different ways, that doesn't mean there aren't facts.'

'I know,' said his new acquaintance, running his hand through his hair. 'That is, of course, the Rationalist position. It is one that I share myself. But it seems to me the issue may have important legal implications. If you take the view that the facts are there and that people – Examining Magistrates, for instance – can discover them, you might take the view that a judge has only to be presented with them for him to be able to reach a verdict. Whereas if you take the view that there are no facts as such but only different versions of them, what the judge has to do is weigh one version against another. The facts are something that is openly decided in court.'

'And this is Hegel's view?' asked Dmitri, looking at the book again.

'Well, no,' confessed the man shyly. 'It is my own. I was going to develop it in my article.'

'Which article was this?'

'The one I was about to write when they sent me to Siberia.'

But did not this mean, thought Dmitri, as he walked away, that the role of the Examining Magistrate was diminished? Dmitri was against anything that diminished the role of Examining Magistrates. True, it enhanced the role of the advocate in Court, and Dmitri was for anything that did that, even though at the moment he was in a subordinate position and had to play second fiddle there to a lot of dopes.

Still, it was an interesting idea. This fellow was a lot more stimulating than his friends in Kursk. Igor Stepanovich, for instance, with his de facto law. De facto indeed! It still rankled. But did the idea have important legal implications, as the chap had said? Surely not. It was merely a question of another way of looking at things. He would put that point the next time they had a discussion.

But just a minute! He wasn't here to have discussions. He was here to find out the facts about Anna Semeonova's disappearance.

And the facts were not at all subjective, they were pretty real, at least as far as Anna Semeonova was concerned.

The facts were – he really must get his mind back to it – that Anna Semeonova had arrived at Tiumen Prison and then disappeared. Almost certainly she had been put, because of her official identification as Marfa Shumin, in one of the cells upstairs reserved for political prisoners. He had missed her before when he had gone through them with the prison official, but he would just have to go through them again.

But how was he going to do that? Even the resourceful Methodosius had been unable to come up with a suggestion. The yard, it appeared, could be of no help this time. The prisoners were up there and the yard was down here.

But hold on! Dmitri stopped in his tracks. The prisoners weren't up there, at least, not all of them. His friend from Kazan, the man he had just been talking to, was a political prisoner and he was down here.

Dmitri hurried back to him.

'You are, of course, a political?'

'Of course!' said the man, surprised.

'Then what are you doing down here? I thought you were kept up in the cells?'

'We're allowed down for exercise.'

'All of you?'

The man looked round.

'Most of us. Of course, some prefer – '

'Women? What happens to the women?'

'They stay up. It's not very nice. Alexandra has complained – '

'So the women are kept up there all the time?'

'Yes.'

'How could I get to see them?'

A look of discomfort crossed the man's face.

'My dear fellow, I must tell you we treat the women with respect. Great respect. It's an absolute law among us. Unwritten, of course.'

'No, no, my intentions are quite – The fact is, I'm looking for a particular woman, Shumin, her name is – '

'Shumin? Someone was asking about her the other day.'

'Yes, I know.'

'Shumin? Wait, I'll certainly ask the others if they know her. But, look, why don't you just come up?'

'Come up?' said Dmitri, flabbergasted.

'Yes. At the end of exercise. They never count. Anyway, if we leave it late, it will be too dark for them to see.'

'But – '

'You can come down the next morning. Of course, you'll have to stay the night.'

'But – '

'You did want to come up?'

'Yes, but – '

When the time came, a small group of men gathered outside one of the doors. They were in ordinary, rather well-to-do clothing, not convict grey, and did not wear chains. They were all chatting happily when Dmitri and his friend arrived. From the tone of the conversation, and its substance, they were all educated men; not very different, in fact, from Dmitri's younger associates at Kursk.

'Can I introduce my friend – incidentally, what *is* your name, my dear fellow? Somehow I seem to have mislaid it.'

'Dmitri.'

'Dmitri. My friend, Dmitri.'

They all shook hands.

'And yours?' muttered Dmitri, as the door opened.

'Grigori. Grigori Pavlinsky.'

They filed inside and began to go up some steps. There were two guards, but they were talking and paid little attention. At the top of the stairs they were met by another guard who led them along the corridor, unlocking each door in turn. At every door some prisoners went in.

'Here we are!' said Grigori.

'Home again, Mr Pavlinksy,' said the guard indulgently, as to a child.

Grigori pushed Dmitri in at the door and crowded in after him. Several others followed. The door swung shut behind them.

'And what,' said the bespectacled man opposite him, 'is your view of the Polish Question?'

'Polish Question?'

'Do you believe the Komskyites should be suppressed or supported?'

'Well ...'

'You pose the antithesis too sharply, Stepan,' another man cut in. 'It is possible to tolerate the Komskyites without either supporting or suppressing them.'

'But isn't that to evade the issue? What do you think?' turning to Dmitri.

'Well ...'

'And are you right to lump the Komskyites together, anyway?' said a third man, joining in enthusiastically. 'What do you think?' he appealed to Dmitri.

'Well ...'

'Well?' They all listened eagerly.

'Who *are* the Komskyites?'

'You don't know?' They seemed very disappointed.

'I expect it's all happened since he came in,' said the bespectacled man to the others. 'Have you been in long?' he said to Dmitri.

'Well, er, no. Not very long.'

'And you didn't see it in the papers?'

'Komskyites? No, I don't think so.'

'Perhaps it wasn't in the papers,' said one of the men dejectedly.

'Oh, surely, it would have been. A mass movement – '

'Not very mass. About fifty. And in Poland, too. They always discriminate against Poland.'

'You didn't see anything at all? No mention of the Komskyite revolt?'

'I'm afraid not.'

'Well, of course, the censorship *is* quite efficient.'

'Are you Poles?' asked Dmitri.

'No, no. Just sympathizers.'

'Actually,' said the bespectacled man, 'it doesn't affect the issue. Is it possible ever to treat a dissident group neutrally? That is the question.'

The question being posed in the abstract, Dmitri felt unhindered by his lack of factual knowledge from joining in. The discussion continued vigorously and it was quite some time before Dmitri could detach himself sufficiently to glance round at his surroundings.

The cell contained some twenty people, both men and women, although mostly men. There was no sleeping platform down the middle, as there had been in the larger barracks he had seen, but there appeared to be some low bunks around the walls. There was one small window, glassed in and kept shut because even so late in the spring the temperature at nights could fall below zero. With all the people in the cell, the air was thick and heavy.

It was also very dark. Dmitri could hardly see the faces of the people he was talking to. Over in one corner, though, there were a couple of candles, beneath an ikon, and by their light Grigori was reading.

A woman came up to Dmitri.

'You're Dmitri, aren't you? Hello, I'm Alexandra.'

They shook hands.

'I'm the librarian.'

'Librarian?'

'We've pooled our books and formed a co-operative library. We can cater for most interests. What are yours?'

'Well, er, well – law!' said Dmitri.

'Law? Oh, that is fortunate! We have quite a good stock in that area. Grigori brought a number of his books with him and there are several lawyers in the other cells. You yourself didn't by any chance bring …'

'I'm afraid not. I, er, left in rather a hurry.'

'Never mind. I'm sure you'll get some sent. We are building our collection up. Would you like to see it?'

She took Dmitri over to where a surprising number of books were arranged on the floor, spine upwards, beside one of the bunks.

'This is the law section.'

'I was looking,' said Dmitri, mindful of his conversations with Grigori, 'for something on the development of Russian law.'

'Legal history?'

'Yes. But understood quite widely. Perhaps even constitutional history?'

'We've certainly got something on that,' said Alexandra, searching. 'But – ' with the eternal voice of the librarian – 'it's out.'

Several of the books were in English. Because of his Scottish background, Dmitri read English quite well. His knowledge of English history, however, was distinctly shaky. Russia had always been closer intellectually to France and Germany. Its aristocracy habitually spoke French, its administrative class, German. This by itself was enough to predispose Dmitri in England's favour, and English history was one of the things he had always meant to read up about.

He was, however, slightly confused about the difference between Scotland and England. Family tradition was clear that they were two different countries and that the English were the enemy. It was because Ancestor Cameron had not been able to accept their rule, so family tradition claimed, that he had left Scotland to take service under the Tsar. On the other hand, family tradition also made it plain that Ancestor Cameron had been an avaricious old bastard and the migration might be explained less nobly but more simply as an attempt to get a better job.

Family tradition was not, then, an altogether clear guide on the subject, and reading might be a better one. But here, too, there were problems. If the Scottish were the oppressed, how was it that they kept turning up in positions of prominence in English society, in law, business, politics and letters? The explanation, and one which Dmitri could identify with, was obviously superior merit. All the same, it was puzzling.

He picked up a book on English constitutional history by Sir Henry Maine. His mind kept going back to the conversation he had had with Grigori about the difference between the constitutional position of law in Russia and that in Western Europe. England, like Russia, was a monarchy. Might not there be some interesting comparisons?

'May I take this one?' he said.

'Please do.'

Alexandra wrote it down in a little pocket book.

'Please bring it back in a fortnight,' she said. 'Or earlier, of course, if you're posted.'

Like the others, she took it for granted that he was a prisoner.

Dmitri bore his book off, pleased. Then his heart smote him. He wasn't here to have a good read! He had come here to find Anna Semeonova.

'Actually, I'm looking for a girl,' he said to Alexandra.

'You are?'

Alexandra brightened.

'Her name is Shumin.'

'Oh!'

'Or possibly something else. Her real name is Semeonova, Anna Semeonova.'

'Really?' said Alexandra distantly.

'I'm pretty sure she's in one of these cells.'

'What did you say her name was?' said Alexandra, relenting slightly. 'I don't remember anyone of that name. What does she look like?'

'Very fair. Almost silvery. A real Russian beauty, as they say.'

'I'm sure there's no one like that. However, I'll have a look the next time I go round.'

'You go round?' said Dmitri incredulously.

'Of course. How else can I be librarian?'

'But —'

'We pay the guards, naturally. They're not very bothered. They don't think books are important,' said Alexandra sniffily.

'Very fair, did you say?' said a man sitting on a bunk nearby. He, too, was reading a book. 'Almost silvery? I saw a girl like that.'

'You did?' said Dmitri delightedly.

'Yes. The other day. Not in the cells, though. In the infirmary.'

'The infirmary?'

'Yes. It's over the road. Next to the women's prison but in a separate building. They isolate the patients. It makes sense, since there's such a risk of epidemics here. It's about the only thing they do,' said the man disgustedly, 'for health reasons.'

He stood up and shook hands.

'Konstantin. I'm a doctor. Not that it makes much difference here, but that's how I came to be in the infirmary. They were short of a doctor. Ordinarily they wouldn't have bothered, but with the numbers – '

'Numbers?' said Dmitri. 'Why?'

'Typhoid.' The doctor shrugged. 'Typhoid fever is endemic here. It's the conditions. And the fact that there's always a population here. The number of cases has increased sharply of late. I would call it an epidemic. They don't.'

'The girl you saw …?'

'Not a patient, no.' The doctor frowned. 'I think she was a kind of orderly. Not one of the regular ones, I got to know them. But an orderly of some kind. I only saw her the once.'

105

'But — very silvery, you said? Age?'

'About twenty. Very competent, I thought. She looked as if she knew her stuff.'

'You didn't catch her name?'

'I'm afraid not.'

It had to be, though, thought Dmitri. The infirmary! That's where she had been all the time. She must have been sent there the moment she had arrived in Tiumen. But why?

'You're sure she wasn't a patient?'

The doctor hesitated.

'She could have been convalescing, I suppose.'

That might be it. The rigours of the journey … a delicate girl … exposure to God knows what. All the same, her name – or the name of Shumin – had not appeared on any of the sick lists. A simple mistake, perhaps? Clerical error – another one? Even Dmitri, though, was beginning to lose his faith in the infinite capacity of the Russian bureaucratic machine to make mistakes. No, the doctor was probably right. She was not there as a patient.

But even if she was there in some other capacity, as an orderly, perhaps, as Konstantin had suggested, her name ought to have appeared somewhere. She couldn't have simply turned up at the infirmary; someone must have sent her. The prison authorities must have known; and if they had known, why were they keeping it hidden?

Released from his cell the next morning, Dmitri was glad to go out into the yard and breathe air. By the time the politicals were allowed downstairs, the yard was already full of grey coats and squashed hats, and heavy with the sound of chains chinking.

Methodosius came across towards him.

'A message for you,' he said, 'from the girls. They want you to go and see them.'

'In the same way?'

'Why not?'

Methodosius was no longer in the fatigues party, but that, he assured Dmitri, presented no problem. He would exchange with someone. And, if one, why not two?'

'It happens all the time,' he said. 'A couple of cigarettes and it's done. And another couple and the guards don't mind.'

It was not as easy, however, to arrange a visit to the infirmary.

'They've got their own orderlies. And since the infirmary is in a block of its own, and further out, they look at you pretty carefully. It's not something I could fix.'

Pressed, however, he said that it might be something that somebody else could fix and that he would see.

Dmitri had to be content with that. For the moment, he turned his mind to other things: the shit-buckets, for instance.

They staggered out with them the next morning. Even empty, they were heavy enough for Dmitri and he was not looking forward to the return. Across the road they went, and through the gate; and then, after a few minutes, into the barracks where he was greeted enthusiastically by the women.

'Isn't he lovely?'

'It suits you, darling!'

'This way, lovey!'

Methodosius had business to attend to at the other end of the hut.

'So?' said Dmitri, sitting down on the edge of the sleeping platform while the women clustered around him.

'That separate party,' they said, 'we know where it went.'

'You do?'

'The infirmary.'

'Ah!'

'And Anya went with them. That's definite. We've spoken with somebody who saw her.'

'You don't know why she was sent to the infirmary?'

'No.'

'She wasn't sick or anything?'

'She didn't look sick,' said the woman who had seen her at the gate, 'not when I saw her.'

'I thought maybe the journey …'

The women laughed.

'Isn't he sweet?'

'They'd have us all in the infirmary, love, if they took that into account!'

'She had it easy,' said someone. 'I saw her riding with the Milk-Drinkers.'

'What was that?'

'With the Milk-Drinkers, love. They often ride on the carts with the sick.'

'That's because they're looking after them,' someone explained. 'They're like that.'

'Was she looking after the sick, too?'

That would make sense of the move to the infirmary.

The women looked at each other.

'She wasn't on the carts at the start,' said someone, 'because she was with us.'

'Ah, yes. But then we got separated. She went off because of that man. I don't think I saw her after that. When was it that you saw her, Liza?'

'Nearly the last day. We came up with a lot of carts and she was in one of them.'

'Perhaps she'd got mixed up with a hospital convoy in between.'

'Did no one else see her?'

The women shook their heads.

'We were further back,' they said. 'It was a long convoy. Several miles.'

'What about the Milk-Drinkers? Are any of them here?'

'Not in this hut. Maybe in one of the other ones.'

'I'll go and look, if you like,' offered one of the women.

But Methodosius was already returning from his labours.

'See what you can find out,' said Dmitri. 'I'll try and come again.'

'Well, girls,' said Methodosius. 'Satisfied?'

'I wouldn't say that.'

'Well, maybe you're too many for him. Maybe he needs some help.'

'Oh, he's not interested in us. His heart's on someone else.'

'A real Russian beauty!'

The guard opened the door. Dmitri and Methodosius went to the bucket and tried to shake it loose. Some of the contents spilled over again and he gagged at the stench.

'Goodbye, girls,' said Methodosius. 'See you again!'

'You can bring him again, too. We haven't given up hope.'

As they were going out of the gate, Dmitri stumbled. The guard pushed him roughly back into line. In doing so, he dislodged Dmitri's convict cap, which was several sizes too large for him, anyhow. Dmitri bent quickly to pick it up. Not quickly enough. The guard caught a glimpse of his face and froze.

'Here!' he said. 'What's this?'

'Nothing,' said Methodosius. 'You've seen nothing. Look, we'll make it all right for you.'

But once inside the gate of the main prison, the guard made them stop. He called into the guard house and guards came running out.

'Just look at this!'

He made Dmitri take his cap off.

'Bloody hell! Carrying the shit-buckets!'

One of the guards went off and returned with the senior official Dmitri knew. He took one look at Dmitri and went pink.

'Dmitri Alexandrovich!'

'All right, all right!' said Dmitri.

'With the buckets!'

'How else?' said Dmitri.

The man swallowed.

'I'm afraid, sir, I shall have to report this.'

'Do so,' said Dmitri.

'I must ask you to come with me.'

It became obvious that he was being taken to the Governor.

'Shall I change first?'

'No, sir,' said the official distantly. 'He must see you as you are.'

'I thought the smell – '

But it was no good. He was paraded before the Governor.

'Dmitri Alexandrovich!'

'Since you will not allow me to perform my duties in ordinary ways,' said Dmitri, 'I have to perform them in other ways.'

'But this – this, sir, is deception!'

'Necessary deception.'

Dmitri, in the wrong and therefore belligerent, wondered for a moment whether to point out that his was not the only deception. Why had the Governor concealed from him that Anna Semeonova was in the infirmary?

'Sir,' spluttered the Governor, 'you have not behaved like a gentleman!'

8

The following morning, Dmitri was summoned to the Governor again.

'I must ask you to leave.'

'I have not completed my inquiries yet,' said Dmitri.

'Your presence has become unwelcome.'

'I am sure of that,' said Dmitri. 'It is not a great pleasure to me either. Nevertheless, I shall stay until I have completed my inquiries.'

'I am afraid you do not have the choice.'

'Oh?' said Dmitri. 'Why not?'

'Siberia is a Restricted Area. You may not enter it, travel in it, or reside in it without special permission.'

'Which I have.'

'And which can be revoked at any time. I propose to revoke it.'

Dmitri considered.

'Is that wise?'

The Governor sat back in surprise.

'Oh, very wise, I would have said.'

'In view of the fact that when I get back to Kursk I shall report that you have obstructed my inquiries.'

'I do not think that will get you far.'

'Oh, I don't think *I* will come into it. The girl's family – a well-connected family, may I say – '

'Yes, I know,' said the Governor: 'Dolgorukov. Well, let me tell you, I've had inquiries made, and Dolgorukov knows nothing about it.'

'Yet,' granted Dmitri. 'The family is waiting for my return. They are expecting me to come back with their daughter. When I don't, I think you can expect quite a lot of people to hear about it, including Prince Dolgorukov. The affair has, after all, aroused widespread interest, The daughter of a well-to-do family, deported to Siberia through bureaucratic incompetence, lost, somehow, at Siberia's leading prison – '

'There is no evidence', said the Governor, stung, 'of the girl's ever having been here!'

'Oh, yes, there is,' said Dmitri. 'Oh, yes, there is!'

The Governor looked at him quickly.

'What evidence?'

'It will appear in my report.'

The Governor sat for a moment or two, thinking.

'I don't believe there is any such evidence,' he said at last.

Dmitri merely smiled.

'As for your charge of obstruction ...'

'The public will, of course, want to know why the authorities at Tiumen found it necessary to resort to obstruction. Was it to cover up administrative error? Or was it ...?'

The Governor flushed.

'You are offensive, sir!'

'I am merely stating the questions that will be asked.'

'I deny that there has been any obstruction!'

'Restriction of access: is not that obstruction?'

'You have been shown every cell there is in the place!'

'Cell, yes.'

'I am afraid I do not understand what you are implying.'

'Aren't there other places where prisoners are?'

'It may surprise you to know, young man,' said the Governor with heavy sarcasm, 'that our policy here is to keep prisoners in prison!'

'What if they're sick?'

'They're put in the infirmary.'

'Well, then …'

'The infirmary', said the Governor crushingly, 'counts as part of the prison.'

'But it is not a part that I have been taken to.'

'That is in your own interest. Disease, infection – '

'Nevertheless, it is a place which I would like to visit.'

The Governor sat looking at him for quite some time.

'I am prepared to consider a written application,' he said at last.

Dmitri thought he had won a kind of victory.

'Here he is again!' said the clerks jovially. 'What is it this time, young Barin?'

Young Barin, or young Lord, was what they called him, confident that they had the Governor's nod not to take him too seriously.

'The sick lists.'

'What, again?'

'Again,' said Dmitri shortly, and settled down to go through them. They ran to a lot of pages. Well, maybe that was not surprising. Many of the prisoners would have been in prison for weeks, perhaps months, before being sentenced, and prisons were not healthy places. Tiumen was not the only prison where typhoid fever was endemic. And then there was the journey itself, which would have borne hard on the weaker prisoners. All the same, there were a lot of them.

He could quite see why they had been glad of the help of the Milk-Drinkers. What did they do when there weren't any, he wondered? Or were there always Milk-Drinkers?

Perhaps, though, there weren't usually as many sick as there had been on this convoy. On an impulse, he asked if he could see the sick lists for previous convoys. With much exaggerated shrugging of shoulders and raising of eyes to the heavens, the clerks produced them from the files. They were appreciably shorter. Was it something to do with the time of year? Dmitri asked if he could see the lists for the corresponding time in previous years. Yet more shrugging.

'We've got other things to do besides look after you, you know.'

Always the sick lists were shorter. The convoy that Anna Semeonova had travelled on had had an unusually large number of sick people.

He looked again at the original list. Some of the names, but only a few, had descriptive entries against them: 'lame', for instance, or 'pregnant'. Description was more common for the earlier names on the list, possibly because the guards had made the entries at the outset to save themselves the trouble of having to re-establish the facts as they went along.

The names were not arranged in alphabetical or any other order. It looked as if a guard had simply gone round collecting names for his list. They appeared to have done this every morning or evening, for there were clear indications when one day's entries ended and another's began. There were a lot of names on the first day – perhaps there had been a general check at the outset in order to assign those unable to walk to carts – and then after that just a few each day until …

On the ninth day there was an unusually long list of entries. None of them had any descriptions against them. There was merely a long list of names.

Dmitri checked again carefully. There was no doubt that they had all been entered at the same time, at the same point in the convoy's progress. Was it simply that someone else had been keeping a separate list, perhaps for a different part of the convoy, and that at that point the lists had been consolidated? Or …

Surely everyone couldn't have fallen ill together! Food poisoning, water? He turned the pages over. There was nothing to indicate why so many had gone down all together. What was it that had happened on the ninth day of the march?

Dmitri applied to the clerks.

'Is a log-book kept of the convoy?'

'Log-book?'

'Daily record of events.'

'There aren't any events on a convoy.'

'Escapes, accidents – '

'There aren't any escapes. And accidents happen all the time.'

'Suppose there was a really big accident; would that be reported?'

The clerks looked at each other.

'I suppose so.'

'Where?'

'A report would go to the Governor, I expect.'

'Is a report regularly made to the Governor when the convoy gets in?'

'I expect so.'

'Can I see it?'

'You'd have to ask the Governor.'

Dmitri went to see the Governor's secretary.

'Report? Oh, yes. First thing when the convoy gets in.'

'In writing?'

'Not always. Not when there's nothing much to report.'

'Was a report made in writing this time?'

The secretary hesitated just long enough for Dmitri to raise his eyebrows.

'Yes.'

'Can I see it?'

'You would have to apply for permission in writing,' said the secretary, recovering.

Dmitri did so. The reply came later that afternoon. Scrawled on his application in the Governor's handwriting were the words: Irrelevant to inquiries. Permission refused.

Dmitri went into the yard to look for Timofei. He found him sitting by himself with his back against the wall.

'Hello,' he said. 'Found your girl yet?'

'Still looking,' said Dmitri. He dropped down beside the Milk-Drinker.

'Timofei,' he said, 'were you on the convoy that's just got in?'

'Yes. About a week ago.'

'That's right. Were you the only Milk-Drinker in the convoy?'

'Oh, no. There were half a dozen of us.'

'How was that?'

'They came to the village and rounded us up.'

'The ones who hadn't paid their taxes?'

'It wasn't quite like that. Not this time. It was those of us who had put our names to a petition.'

'What was the petition?'

'It was asking for the release of the elders. They had come to the village before, see, and taken the elders, or most of them, when we were refusing to pay our taxes. I was about the only one left. So this time they took me. And the women who'd put their names to the petition. It had to be women, see, because they were about the only ones who were left. Bar me.'

There were quite a lot of points here that Dmitri wanted to take up. Arresting people for not paying their taxes he could see, just; but merely for signing a petition? If that, of course, was all they had done. He would have liked to have given them some legal advice. These people were plainly in need of a lawyer. He would have to come back to it with Timofei. However, he mustn't allow himself to be sidetracked.

'So, the other Milk-Drinkers on the convoy were all women?'

'Yes. We were all sentenced together,' said Timofei benignly. He seemed completely philosophical about the whole thing, as if it was something to be endured, not resisted. Or perhaps he had resisted? Perhaps his way of resisting was not paying taxes.

Again, there were points here that Dmitri would have liked to take up. However...

'Were you with the women on the convoy?'

'At first, yes. We all walked together singing psalms to keep our spirits up. But then they wanted to separate us. They said it wasn't decent to have the women with the men. But I said that Marya had just had a baby and needed help. Then they said if I was her husband, we'd all better travel with the family convoy. And I said I wasn't her husband. Then they said what the hell was I to do with it in that case? And I said we were all bidden to help one another. And then the guards told the sergeant not to bother about it, that I was a Milk-Drinker and wouldn't be a nuisance. So they let me go on with the women.'

'And you stayed with them all the time?'

'Well, no, because one day, quite late in the journey, they came along and said there'd been a bit of an accident, and would the Milk-Drinking women mind going along and giving a hand. Well, of course they wouldn't mind, that's what God put us here for, isn't it? And the women were used to nursing the sick, so off they went, including Marya and the baby, and there wasn't any need for me. So back I went to join the men.'

'And you didn't see the women again?'

'No. They'll be over in the women's prison.'

'And you didn't hear any more about this accident?'

'No, not a thing. I thought I might – news travels along a convoy, after all, and I wanted to hear how the women were getting on – but I didn't hear a word. Haven't heard a word since, either.'

Dmitri had submitted a request to visit the infirmary. Back that came, too. On it was written.

Permission refused. Contagious diseases.

'No, I can't,' said Methodosius. 'It's not like getting into the women's prison. Besides, they're after me now.'

Support, though, came from Timofei.

'He knows she's there,' he said.

'And I can't get in there any other way,' said Dmitri.

'It's just across the road. Give him a hand.'

Methodosius began to weaken.

'I'd have to have some help,' he said.

'What sort of help?'

Methodosius did not reply.

'It'll cost you money,' he said.

'How much money?'

'More than a few cigarettes.'

The next day, however, when he came up to Dmitri in the yard, he said:

'It's not just money.'

'No?'

'They want to talk to you. They won't do it without.'

'Well, I don't mind talking. Who are "they"?'

'It's the Artel.'

'The Artel? What's that?'

'Well, it's – it's like what they have in some of the big firms. A sort of workers' co-operative. They all get together.'

'A trade union?'

'Yes, yes. Like that. Sort of.'

'They all get together to defend their interests?'

'Yes. You could say that. Yes.'

'Well, that's all right. I don't mind talking to them.'

'Yes. Well. Good. It's … it's not altogether like a trade union.'

'No?'

'No. I mean, well, it's prisoners, you see.'

'Well, that's all right. I can see the Government might not recognize it, but then it's not going to recognize some of the things I do, either.'

'Too true. But – '

'I don't mind talking to them.'

'The question is,' said Methodosius, 'whether they mind talking to you.'

'Oh. You mean because I'm an Examining Magistrate?'

'Is that what you are?' said Methodosius, looking unhappy.

'Perhaps we'd better just say "lawyer".'

Methodosius was silent.

'Well, it's too late now, isn't it?' said Dmitri impatiently. 'They know I'm a lawyer already. I said I was at the gate. You know, that time – '

'Yes, I know. As a matter of fact, that's why they might be willing to see you.'

'*Because* I'm a lawyer, you mean?'

'Yes. Only, you see, they want to know what kind of lawyer you are. I mean, are you an Examining Magistrate kind of lawyer, or are you – well, you did speak up at the gate, didn't you? The point is, before they'd agree to do anything like this – it's crazy, isn't it, I mean? – they'd want to be sure about the sort of lawyer you are.'

'I don't know what kind of lawyer I am,' said Dmitri.

'Well, that's just it. That's how they feel too. So they want to make sure. They want to talk to you first.'

'I don't mind that.'

'No. Well. Perhaps not. Only …' He fished around for words. 'The thing is – look, I'll try to get them to promise that they'll leave you alone, even if they don't like you, but the thing is – ' he looked despairingly at Timofei for help – 'they're not the sort of blokes, see, who would always keep their promise.'

'Oh. I see,' said Dmitri.

Nevertheless, he agreed; and the following night the meeting took place.

It took place after dark when all the prisoners were supposed to be in their barracks. The yard was indeed deserted when Dmitri came down. He stood for a moment uncertainly. Then a figure detached itself from the wall.

'Right?' said Methodosius.

He took Dmitri across to one of the huts. The door was supposed to be locked. It wasn't.

Inside, the room was full of men, some lying on the sleeping platform, others squatting on the ground playing cards. The room was lit by two oil lamps, one at each end of the sleeping platform. Most of the men were clustered at the nearest end. Methodosius led Dmitri to the other end.

A small group of men was sitting talking. On the sleeping platform between them was a jug of vodka. They looked up as Methodosius and Dmitri approached.

'This him?'

Methodosius nodded.

Most of the men got up and moved away, leaving just two of them. One had a large scar running diagonally across his face. The other had two scars, one running one way, one, the other, so that they formed a large X. Dmitri knew he had not seen the men before and yet their faces seemed vaguely familiar. After a moment he worked out why. They were the sort of faces he saw every week in the Court House at Kursk; on their way to prison.

One of the men motioned to Dmitri to sit down. Methodosius hesitated, then sat down too. The men looked at him. He fidgeted nervously but stayed.

They turned their attention to Dmitri and sat looking at him for a long time in silence.

'He looks like a political,' one of them said at last.

'He can't help the way he looks,' said Methodosius.

'I don't like politicals.'

'He's all right,' said Methodosius, beginning to perspire slightly. 'I know him.'

'How long have you known him?'

'He helped me at the gate,' said Methodosius, evading the issue.

'We know that.'

They continued to inspect Dmitri in silence.

'What are you doing here?' one of them asked suddenly.

'I'm looking for a girl.'

'Bollocks!'

Dmitri shrugged.

'You asked; I've told you.'

'He really is,' put in Methodosius.

'Shut up!'

They continued to study Dmitri.

'What's her name?' asked one of them unexpectedly.

Dmitri hesitated.

'That's a bit complicated, actually. Her real name is Anna Semeonova. But she's here under the name of Shumin.'

That didn't seem to bother them. Perhaps they were used to people appearing under different names.

'She a political or something?'

'I hate politicals,' said the other one.

'Shumin's a political; she's not.'

'You've lost me,' said the more reasonable-seeming one, the man with a single scar. 'Are there two of them?'

'No. Shumin escaped. The other one somehow got sent in her place.'

'To Siberia?'

'Yes.'

'How was that, then?'

'I don't know how it happened. That's what I'm here to find out. I think,' said Dmitri cautiously, 'it may simply have been a mistake.'

'Mistake?'

'Yes.'

'She got sent to Siberia by mistake?' said the single-scarred man incredulously.

'I think so.'

'Look, mate,' said Single-scar definitely, 'people don't get sent to Siberia by mistake! The bloody Tsar knows what he's doing!'

'One would have thought so, but – '

'He talks like a political,' said Double-scar. 'I hate politicals.'

'Why don't you shut up?' said Dmitri.

The man's face went hard.

'This girl got sent out by mistake?' said the other man, disregarding him.

'I think so. She was in the prison yard at Kursk and the guards put her on a cart thinking she was – '

Single-scar turned to Double-scar.

'Believe it?' he said.

'Not a word!'

'I know it sounds incredible – '

'It bloody does!'

'He talks like a political,' said Double-scar. 'I hate politicals.'

'For Christ's sake!' said Dmitri. 'Don't you have any other ideas in your thick head?'

'I'm getting pissed off with you,' said the man, beginning to stand up.

'Well, I'm getting pissed off with you, too,' said Dmitri, also rising.

The man put his hand in his pocket.

'Easy, now,' said Methodosius quickly.

The knife came out.

Methodosius caught the man's arm.

With incredible speed the man transferred the knife to his other hand and slashed at Methodosius.

Dmitri hit him.

The lamp on the sleeping platform went out. The lamp at the other end of the hut went out too. In its last flicker, Dmitri saw men standing up all over the place, their knives out.

Then the hut was plunged into darkness.

Someone – Methodosius – caught him by the arm and began to drag him towards the door. They blundered into someone and pushed him aside. Dmitri felt a sharp kick on the shins. Then they ran into a whole knot of men and couldn't get further.

Methodosius began to move again, this time sideways. They came up against the wall and began to feel their way along it.

Suddenly, somehow, a lamp came on. Everywhere there was a struggling mass of men. And there, right beside him, were the men from the Artel.

'Don't do it!' cried Methodosius desperately. 'He's an innocent!'

The knife stopped.

'Innocent?'

'Yes, he's simple. Simple as a child. He didn't mean anything by it!'

'It's unlucky to knife an innocent, Ivan!' said someone worriedly.

Other voices joined in, in support.

'You can't do that!'

'It's all wrong!'

The knife was lowered.

'Well, how was I to know he was an innocent?' grumbled Double-scar.

'He can't be that much of an innocent,' said Single-scar. 'He's a lawyer, isn't he?'

'Well, that's what you want, isn't it?' cried Methodosius. 'You wanted a lawyer! And then when one comes along you try and stick a knife in him!'

The two men looked at each other.

'You wanted a lawyer,' said Methodosius, pressing home his advantage. 'Well, now you've bloody got one. Why don't you get on and talk to him, for Christ's sake?'

The single-scarred man nodded slowly. He sat down on the platform again, reached out and pushed the jug of vodka towards Dmitri.

'Have a drink,' he said.

Some time – and quite a lot of vodka – later, relations had become very warm.

'I wouldn't have cut him!' said Double-scar tearfully.

'Of course you wouldn't!' Single-scar reassured him. 'How were you to know?'

'It's because he talks like a political. I never could understand those buggers.'

'They're a funny lot,' Methodosius agreed pacifically, inspecting the jug and finding it, to his surprise, empty. Dmitri hoped the big man was not going to pass out.

'They get up my nose,' said Double-scar. 'I mean, what are they doing out here, anyway? I mean, it's not as if they've done anything. I mean, you sit down here next to anyone and you get talking and you find he's hit some rich merchant on the head. Well, that's something, isn't it? I mean, you say to yourself, here's a man who's done something. But you never find a political like that. There's nothing to them. What have they ever done in life?'

'It takes all sorts to make a world,' said Methodosius, still pacific.

And still thirsty. He picked up the jug and looked around. Someone took it from him and returned it full. Where they got the drinks from, Dmitri did not know. It appeared that the usual prison laws did not apply to the Artel.

'And that's very true,' said Double-scar, much struck. 'But what I'm saying is, politicals are not like the rest of us. You can't trust them.'

Dmitri hastily filled the man's mug.

'Thanks. You're not a bad sort, even though you're a bit simple. Where was I? Oh, yes, politicals. Well, as I say, you can't trust them. Take this recent business, for instance. Now I'm not against having a go at the guards, right? Sometimes they ask for it and you wait until they're on their own one dark night and then you let them have it. But that's different, isn't it, from putting others up to it? Putting them up to it and egging them on and then keeping out of it yourself? I don't call that right.'

'I don't call it right, either,' said Dmitri firmly. But hazily. What was it that he was not calling right?

'No. And I'm with you there. And what I'm saying is, it was poor sods like us who got put up while the politicals stayed out of it. Put us up and then stayed out of it. I don't call that fair, and that's what I've got against politicals. They're a sneaky lot!'

'Takes all sorts,' muttered Methodosius indistinctly, descending fast.

'And so it does. And what I say is ...' He lost his thread and looked around in puzzlement. 'Jesus, what is it I say?'

He put his head down on his arms and followed Methodosius into insensibility.

That left Single-scar and, surprisingly, Dmitri. But then Dmitri had been talking so much that he had not been giving the same attention to the vodka jug as the others had.

'He's got it in for politicals,' he said thickly.

Single-scar embraced him affectionately.

'He doesn't mean anything by it,' he said. 'It's just his way.'

'Why's he got it in for politicals?' demanded Dmitri, drunkenly belligerent and reluctant to abandon offence.

'Well, he didn't like this recent business. People were used. He says that's the trouble with politicals. They get some idea and everyone else has to jump to it.'

'Yes,' said Dmitri, head swimming. 'Bastards!'

Belligerence gave a last flare.

'Bastards! Bastards!' he shouted, and tried to stand up.

Single-scar pulled him down.

'Have a drink!'

He poured and missed.

'You're drunk!' said Dmitri.

'No I'm not!' said Single-scar indignantly. He pointed at Double-scar and Methodosius. 'They're drunk!' he said, and cackled.

'That's right!' said Dmitri, giggling. 'They're drunk. The bastards!'

What was it, through the mists, that he had come to this place for? Something to do with a woman? What woman was it? Dmitri for the life of him couldn't remember. Vera Samsonova, was it? Flat as a board! He giggled again.

'He just doesn't like politicals,' said Single-scar, still, at a distance, roughly in touch.

'Why's that, then?'

'It's this recent business.'

The mists momentarily receded.

'Recent business? What business is this?'

'What we want to talk to you about. You're a lawyer, aren't you?'

'Yes,' said Dmitri thickly. 'Bloody good one!'

'Knew that! Knew it as soon as I saw you. Well, then.'

'I'm your man!' said Dmitri enthusiastically. Then, as through a gap in the clouds: 'What for?'

'They're all there. You'll see them. You'll know what to do.'

'Dead right,' said Dmitri. The clouds now, however, began to swirl disconcertingly. The gap, if there had been one, was moving sharply away. In it, though, suddenly appeared a word.

'Where?'

'The infirmary. They're all there.'

The infirmary! The gap gave a lurch. That was what he was here for! Anna Semeonova! That's where she was.

'I've got to get there,' he said.

'We'll look after that.'

'That's where she is.'

Single-scar looked at him curiously.

'Are you really after a girl?'

'Yes.'

'Well bugger me!' He reached for the jug. 'What's she like, then?'

'Who?'

'This girl of yours.'

'Beautiful!' said Dmitri. 'Beautiful!'

'The bitch! What's she doing here?'

'Don't know,' said Dmitri, now totally befuddled.

'Got into a scrape, has she? Well that's the way with bitches.'

'Dead right,' said Dmitri. 'Bitches!'

'They're all the same!'

'So they are! Bastards!' shouted Dmitri.

'Bastards!' echoed the single-scarred man, looking about him confusedly.

'I hate politicals!' shouted Dmitri, as his head fell forward on to the platform.

9

When Dmitri came to he found himself in the prison yard lying propped against the wall. It was the next morning, and quite well on into the morning judging by the number of people in the yard. They must have brought him out at first light and put him here.

Dmitri sat up sharply. What if the guards had seen him lying here? He would have some explaining to do.

'Easy on, Barin,' said someone soothingly. 'You're not yourself yet.'

There was a group of men clustered round him, shielding him, he suddenly realized, from the gaze of unwanted onlookers. He looked up at the faces and thought he recognized some of them from the night before. The faces of the men from the Artel were not among them; nor was that of Methodosius.

'The guards!' he said, trying to scramble to his feet.

Someone helped him.

'Don't worry about that, Barin. We've taken care of them.'

Barin! They were all calling him Barin, even the prisoners.

He swayed unsteadily on his feet.

'You go up to your room, Barin, and have a nice lie-down.'

They helped him to the door and he just about made it up the stairs. Then he collapsed on his bed and let the room steady its swirling.

My God, this was terrible. How had he got himself into this situation? An Examining Magistrate, drinking with prisoners, collapsing into insensibility and then allowing himself to be carried out unconscious into the yard! Dmitri was mortified. If the authorities found out about this, he would never recover. Jesus, what a lunatic!

It was all in the pursuit of his inquiries … He could imagine himself saying that – and could imagine the reception! Is that how you carry out your inquiries, Examining Magistrate Kameron?

Only if I have to, and in this case I had to. The prison author-ities were not co-operating. He could imagine the stony faces. We can understand that, Examining Magistrate Kameron!

The face of the prison Governor came before him. Jesus, it was playing into his hands! He would be able to deport Dmitri now and no one would raise an eyebrow. The guards must have seen him lying there.

But had they? The prisoners had said they'd taken care of that, but how could they? Well, perhaps they could. They might simply have shielded him with their bodies. But could he rely on that? Jesus, it was getting worse. He was relying on convicts now! What sort of Examining Magistrate was that?

Someone else had asked that question recently. Methodosius! He had said that was what the Artel wanted to know: What sort of lawyer was he? What had they meant? Bribable? Definitely not! Drunk and incapable? On the evidence, alas … Dmitri lifted his head indignantly. Drunk he might be, but not incapable. Never!

And anyway, that had not been the point of the question. The question was whose side was he on? The Governor's, or …? Dmitri would always have said he was on nobody's side; he was committed solely to the truth. He was an investigating lawyer, not one of those specious rhetorical ones he had seen so often in the Court House at Kursk. He was there to get at the truth, no matter how unacceptable it was and for whom.

So whose side was he on? The Governor's or the yard's? Dmitri thought malevolently of the Governor and was tempted to plump for the yard. But that would not do. He was on no one's side. The law stood apart from sides. It was independent, external and objective.

Or was it? Not in Russia, if his friend upstairs in the cells was correct. Law in Russia, or, at least in Siberia, was the Governor's law, it was what the Tsar or his representatives decreed. According to Grigori, the problem with Russian law was precisely that it wasn't above and independent of the state. Dmitri, interested in ideas, had thought vaguely that this was something he must look into when he got back to Kursk. He was beginning to think now that he would have to look into it rather sooner than he had thought.

The cell was crowded. There were faces here that Dmitri was sure he had not seen before. Others beside himself, and apart from the normal inmates of the cell, must have been invited to Alexandra's party.

On the far side of the room he could hear a new, harsh, unpleasant voice raised in dispute.

'No, no, no, what we need is a truly *scientific* analysis. We must look at the historico-economic bases and find out the scientific laws that determine them. Only then can we achieve a genuinely objective, materialist explanation.'

Dmitri had not come across *him* before, and if he had anything to do with it wouldn't come across him again. One thing he couldn't stand was the mechanistic jargon so fashionable in some radical circles.

He looked around for someone more congenial and saw the doctor he had met on his last visit. He was talking to a middle-aged, rather worn but still pretty woman.

'Lara Kovalevskaya – Dmitri Alexandrovich!'

They shook hands.

'A lovely idea of Alexandra's, isn't it? To have this party? And so typical of her, to want to cheer everyone up!'

'It's her birthday,' said Konstantin, the doctor.

'What a place to celebrate it!' said Dmitri.

'The important thing, though,' said Lara, 'is to celebrate it.'

'That's right,' said Konstantin. 'The one thing you mustn't do is give in.'

Dmitri muttered something about her being an impressive lady. Ordinarily he would have run a mile from someone like Alexandra. He distrusted anyone who tried to organize him. Here, though, he could see that there was a need for people like that. The idea of a party had given everyone a lift and they were all chattering away as excitedly and obliviously as they had once done in the drawing rooms of St Petersburg.

And that was without alcohol! The political prisoners did not appear to have the same ability to command resources as the Artel did. Russian intellectuals, however, reflected Dmitri, did not need alcohol to become intoxicated.

All over the cell, animated discussions were taking place.

'What I am demanding, of course, is a New Positivism.'

God, it was that man again.

Someone pushed a drink into his hand. He sipped it. It was tea. That might not be a bad thing in the circumstances. He was still feeling fragile from his encounter with the Artel. The thought of the Artel put an idea in his head.

'Did you see any Milk-Drinkers when you were over in the infirmary?' he asked Konstantin.

'Milk-Drinkers? I don't think so. Why?'

'The girl I am looking for, the one I was telling you about, was on the hospital carts with some Milk-Drinkers. I wondered if they'd all been taken to the infirmary to help with the nursing.'

'I didn't see any. The medical orderlies were ordinary prison staff. There could, of course, have been other wards.'

'I thought they may have called in other help, the way they called you in.'

'The wards were full, certainly. Every bed was taken. People were even lying on the floor between the beds.'

'That would be because of the big influx from the latest convoy?'

'No, I don't think so. The patients I saw had mostly been there for some time. They were recovering from typhoid fever.'

'I had the impression a lot of patients came in with the latest convoy.'

'Not as far as I know. Of course, I wasn't there when the convoy arrived. I only went there after. Actually,' said Konstantin, thinking, 'that may explain it. Explain my being called in, I mean. Maybe there *were* a lot of extra patients as a result of the convoy and the usual doctors were busy with them.'

'You've no idea what they could have been suffering from?'

'The ones from the convoy? No, as I was saying, I didn't really see any of them. My cases were all typhoid.'

He looked at Dmitri.

'You're thinking there could have been an outbreak of something else? On the journey?'

'They had to call in extra help.'

'That would explain it, of course. Them making use of a separate ward, if that's what they did. Especially if it was infectious. And perhaps that's where the ordinary doctors were.'

'Might the people who had been nursing them on the convoy be there too?'

'Well, they might,' said Konstantin doubtfully. 'I suppose that reduces the risk of spreading infection. All the same … I mean, they're not trained nurses, are they? And it hardly seems ethical to – '

'Ethical?' said Lara. 'You think that would enter into it?'

Alexandra came pushing through the crowd carrying a jug of tea, Russian tea, not black but gold. She brightened when she saw Dmitri.

'Hello,' she said. 'I'm so glad you could come!'

It seemed so incongruous that Dmitri almost laughed. For Alexandra, however, it was clearly not a laughing matter, and Dmitri was oddly touched. She was so determined to keep up, even here, the forms of civilization, the things that made the difference between man and brute. Dmitri was all for that. In his small way that's exactly what he was trying to do at Kursk.

'Happy Birthday!' he said, kissing her warmly. Konstantin and Lara kissed her, too.

He gave her the book which he had brought with him from Kursk. Alexandra, pleased, took it from him and examined it.

'Why, it's a novel!'

'Is that allowed?'

'Yes, of course. We have too many serious books here.'

'This isn't serious?'

Alexandra looked at him.

'You think I'm too much the librarian?'

'I think the idea of having a party is absolutely marvellous!'

Alexandra flushed and turned away.

'There's someone I'd like you to meet,' she said over her shoulder.

Unfortunately, it was the man with the voice.

'Gasparov,' he said, not bothering to look at Dmitri but sticking out a hand in his direction.

Dmitri did not take it.

'I'm sure you two will get on together,' said Alexandra, not noticing. 'You're both men of ideas.'

'What sort of ideas?' said Gasparov suspiciously.

'Does one have to have a sort?' asked Dmitri.

'Certainly,' said Gasparov. 'There has to be consistency to one's intellectual framework.'

'I prefer a generally critical approach, myself,' said Dmitri.

'Hegelian?'

'Kantian,' said Dmitri, casting around.

'Kant,' said Gasparov, 'is passé. He has been superseded.'

'Oh yes? Who by?'

'Hegel. And we,' said Gasparov complacently, 'have superseded Hegel. Hegel was an idealist. We are Materialist. We have taken Hegel and stood him on his head.'

'It seems a very strange position from which to view the world.'

Gasparov recognized at last that he had an adversary.

'So,' he said, 'you are a Pre-Materialist?'

'Certainly not,' said Dmitri coldly. 'I am not an Ist at all.'

'Categorization is the beginning of Reason. You would deny Reason, then?'

'Just your kind of Reason.'

'There is only one kind of Reason: Scientific Reason.'

'Well …'

'It must be so. Science's laws are universal.'

'In the field of Nature, perhaps.'

'In the field of Society, too.'

'And you have discovered them?'

'Are discovering them. Our task, though, is not to discover Society but to change it. For that we need a new Philosophy, a new Positivism, a new – '

'Dogmatism?' suggested Dmitri.

Their neighbours pulled them apart.

'I knew you'd get on,' said Alexandra happily.

There were some more letters for him. He picked them up with an avidity that surprised him. He had never previously supposed that anything that happened in Kursk could possibly interest him. Seen from Siberia, however, even Kursk had its points.

'Dear Dmitri,' Igor Stepanovich wrote, 'there have been some unexpected changes here. Peter Ivanovich has been transferred to another post. So has Novikov. So, even more surprisingly, has Porfiri Porfirovich, you know, the man who chairs the Special Tribunal. It all happened very quickly. One day they were here, the next day they weren't.'

'I just wanted to know', wrote Sonya, 'whether you have detected any signs of spiritual growth yet? You mustn't feel discouraged if you haven't. They will come, Dmitri, I assure you. All the books say so. Just don't harden your heart, Dmitri. Otherwise it will take years.'

'Dear Dmitri,' wrote Vera Samsonova, 'I am writing only to keep you informed. You may remember that in my last letter I mentioned a demonstration that had occurred outside a local tannery. Well, I have had a chance to speak to some of the demonstrators. One of them had fallen ill – the conditions in the prison are appalling – and demanded to see a woman doctor. I asked them about Marfa Shumin. It certainly seems to be the same one. So I asked them why she was prepared to see an innocent woman go to Siberia instead of her.

'Well, they hummed and hawed. Some said that it was right for Anna Semeonova to sacrifice herself since Marfa Shumin was worth more to the cause. I said, that wasn't the point. The point was, was it right for Shumin to sacrifice someone *else* for the cause. They seemed to think, I'm afraid, that it was. What did I expect Shumin to do? they asked. Give herself up? No, I said, just come out with a public statement that she is free and someone else has gone to Siberia in her place.

'They didn't seem to think that was likely, but promised to try and get a message to Shumin. And, you know, Dmitri, I think they may have done, for some funny things have happened here. Peter Ivanovich has been moved and so has Novikov. So has the Chairman of the Special Administrative Tribunal that actually sentenced her.

'Of course, it could simply just be that it has taken all this time for Prince Dolgorukov to find out that there is a place called Kursk, where some funny things have been going on ...'

Methodosius appeared to be in trouble again. A guard was calling out names and men were lining up in front of the gatehouse. Methodosius was among them.

'What's this?' Dmitri asked Timofei.

'Oh, it's nothing,' the Milk-Drinker assured him. 'They're just looking for vodka, that's all.'

Some forty men had lined up.

'They won't find anything,' said Timofei. 'They never do.'

Methodosius, certainly, seemed unconcerned.

The guard had begun a roll call. As each man's name was called out he took one step forward, said, 'Yes, Your Honour', and stepped back into line. Dmitri watched, not exactly with interest, but not idly either. Roll calls were in a way at the heart of this case and he wanted to see again how they were done.

There was something odd about some of the names. He listened more attentively. A surprising number of the men were called, or claimed to be called, Nepomyashchi: Don'tremember. There was an Ivan Don'tremember, a Mustapha Don'tremember, a Fritz Don'tremember, an Abram Don'tremember and several Don'tremembers from down in the Caucasus somewhere.

'Don'tremember?' said Dmitri.

'They don't like to give their real names,' said Timofei.

'But surely the authorities know them?'

He couldn't recollect ever seeing a Don'tremember on a prison list at Kursk. The Court wouldn't have stood for any of that nonsense! Prisoners were charged under their proper names.

'Well, no, they don't.'

'They must have been on their original papers.'

'And were, Excellency, and were!' butted in a prison official who was standing nearby. Strictly speaking, he shouldn't be saying anything to Dmitri, but he couldn't stand by and allow slights to be cast on the administration.

'You see, Your Excellency, these are returners.'

'Returners?'

'Yes. They passed through our hands once and were sent on to camps in Further Siberia. But then the rascals escaped and set off on their way home. Well, it's all right when you're out on the steppe and there's no one about only you and the partridges, but here in the west we've got patrols out and not many get through, I can tell you! They get picked up and brought here.

'So you see, Your Excellency,' continued the official confidently, 'that's how it is they don't have papers. Their documents are in the camps they were sent to out in Further Siberia. And we can't match them up with them because they won't tell us their names, the rascals!'

'Surely there is a list of people who have escaped, isn't there? And couldn't you find a match, for some of them at any rate, by description?'

'But, Excellency, there are so many of them!'

'So many of them?'

'Well, yes, Excellency, look at all these Don'tremembers here!'

'Why won't they give their names?'

'So that we won't know how long they were sentenced to. It's not worth the bother of finding out, you see, Your Excellency, so what we do is simply give them all five years.'

'And that's worth it, is it? Five years!'

'Between you and me, Your Excellency, it's worth it for quite a lot of them.'

He came out and stood beside Dmitri in a companionable way, instructions about keeping distance forgotten.

'The fact is, Your Excellency, some of them make quite a career of it.'

'Of what?'

'Escaping. Yes, I know it sounds odd. But some of them get into the way of it. No sooner are they in than they're out. They're like gypsies, you see, Your Excellency. That's where they like to be, out on the steppe, with the wind blowing and the great sky above. All right, in the end it comes to nothing, because sooner or later they'll get picked up. None of them's ever going to get back to Mother Russia. But I don't think that bothers them, really, because deep down that's not what they're looking for. They just want to be out on the steppe with the wind in their face and the sun on their back. They're wanderers, Your Excellency, that's what they are: wanderers.'

Methodosius was a Don't remember.

When the roll call was completed, the prisoners were left standing there while the guards went into the huts. Methodosius said afterwards that they had turned everything over. They had not found anything, nor, of course, had they expected to. The search was intended, Dmitri suspected, merely to remind the Artel that things could get awkward if the guards weren't paid off. After a while the guards returned empty-handed but unbothered and the line was dismissed.

Methodosius came towards him.

'There's been a bit of a hitch,' he said.

'Hitch?'

'Yes. Over your visit to the infirmary. The visit's still on – it'll be tomorrow night – but they can't find this girl of yours.'

'It could be a mistake, I suppose,' said Dmitri, disappointed.

'No, no, she seems to be there all right. But not under the name you gave.'

'Shumin?'

'That's right.'

'Her real name's Semeonova.'

And then, as that didn't seem to register either:

'The women called her Anya.'

'Yes, that's the one. She seems to be there, all right. But there's some bother about the name.'

'Well, yes, you could certainly say that.'

'Basically, it's: If you want to see Shumin, you can't, but if you want to see Anya, you can.'

'I'm not following this,' said Dmitri. 'They're the same person.'

'Well, I'm not following this either. All I know is, you've got to say which it is you want to see: Shumin or Anya?'

'Well, Anya, of course.'

'All right, then. That should be OK.'

Methodosius went off, leaving Dmitri bewildered.

The following night, however, things went ahead. Shortly after midnight Dmitri descended the stairs from his room and emerged into the yard. Despite the lateness of the season a thin, powdery snow had fallen and covered the yard. Snow was still sifting down. On his face the flakes seemed slight flecks, but against the lantern in the yard they seemed big spots, as if it intended to snow seriously.

Two men slipped out of the shadows and fell in alongside him.

'This way, Your Excellency.'

They led him not towards the main gate but to a little gate in one of the side walls. It was slightly ajar and all they had to do was pull it open and then close it again, almost, behind them.

They walked across the road, their feet crunching in the snow. Dmitri was worried about the noise; worried, too, about the footprints they would leave. The snow was still falling heavily. Perhaps it would cover their tracks. The men didn't seem bothered.

They went up the road, past the women's prison and then on to a smaller, palisaded building that Dmitri had not really taken in before. The men went straight round to the back of the building and found a door, open as the previous one had been. They went through. The building, a large wooden one, was just ahead of them.

The men looked at each other, for the first time uncertain. Then one of them approached the wall of the building and began working his way along it.

He stopped and signalled. They went over to join him. There was a chink between the logs through which came a faint, yellowy light. Dmitri bent down and looked through.

Inside were beds, arranged in separate rows. There were tables beside some of the beds and on the tables were candles. On one table someone was lighting up an old silvery ikon. There were other ikons about the place but he couldn't see them as well. Beside the one he could see, a man was lying in a bed. His chest and head were heavily bandaged and he was holding a crucifix in his hands. Dmitri could now see the other beds. There were people in them, all bandaged.

One of the men with him tapped lightly on the logs. When nothing happened, he tapped again.

There came an answering tap further along the wall. One of Dmitri's companions moved towards it. In the darkness Dmitri could just make out his hand, beckoning.

He went to join him. The chink here was bigger.

Dmitri bent down and looked. Through the chink he saw a mass of silvery blonde hair.

'Anna Semeonova?'

There was a sharp intake of breath on the other side.

'Who are you?'

'Kameron,' he said. 'Examining Magistrate at the Court House at Kursk. You saw me there. We spoke, if you remember.'

'What are you doing here?'

'Looking for you.'

There was a long silence.

'I don't understand,' she said. 'Why are you coming like this? Working with … them?'

'I had to. Look, I'll explain later. What I wanted to do was establish that you were here. It's been difficult – '

'What do you want?' said the girl.

'Want? To get you out, of course. To take you back to Kursk.'

'How do I know?'

'How do you know? Well, for God's sake, you can recognize me, can't you? Can you see me through the hole?' Dmitri moved his head back and let the light play on his face. 'You can recognize my voice. You know who I am. What else would I be doing?'

There was another long silence, so long that he applied his eye again to the chink and saw again the mass of silvery blonde hair.

'How can I be sure?'

Dmitri was taken aback. What else would he be doing? She must be daft or something. Then he upbraided himself. Not daft, but confused. Understandably, quite understandably, confused. Who wouldn't be? After all these weeks. And after all that had no doubt happened to her. And then the circumstances! Dead of night, a man at a hole in the wall claiming to be Examining Magistrate at the Court House at Kursk!

'Look, I know what you must have been through – '

'Do you?' she said. 'Do you?'

'I've got a pretty good idea. But it's all over now. You can come back with me – '

'How do I know it's not a trap?'

'Trap? Why should it be a trap?'

She did not answer. At least, not directly. Instead, she said:

'Who are you? Who did you say you were?'

'Dmitri Kameron. Examining Magistrate at Kursk. You met me, if you remember.'

'Whose side are you on?'

'Whose side am I on?'

It was that question again. Only this time, Dmitri knew, he would have to answer it differently from the way he had done to himself when deliberating in the seclusion of his room.

'You can trust me,' he said.

'But can I?' she said. 'After …'

'You have been through some terrible things. All that is now at an end. I am here to take you home to your parents. You are quite safe with me.'

Again there was a silence.

'Who did you say you were?'

Oh, God, thought Dmitri. What's happened to her?

'Kameron. Dmitri Kameron. You met me – '

'No, no,' she said. 'The other bit.'

'Examining Magistrate? The Court House at Kursk?'

This time she didn't say anything for so long that he looked again to see if she was still there.

'I've come to take you home,' he said gently.

'No,' she said firmly. 'It's better if I stay here.'

'Anna Semeonova!'

'I'm not Anna Semeonova. Not any more.'

'Shumin, then …'

'Nor Shumin either. Least of all, Shumin.'

'Then …?'

'I'm Marya Serafimovna now. Yes, Marya Serafimovna.'

Dmitri left, convinced she was off her head.

10

'Marya Serafimovna?' said Timofei. 'But – '

'Well?' said the Scarfaces eagerly.

'Well, what?' said Dmitri ungraciously. He needed to think things over.

'You saw them, didn't you?'

'Saw who?'

'Them in the ward.'

Dmitri considered. He had certainly seen some people in the ward.

'I saw them, yes.'

'So?'

'So what?'

'Bandages,' prompted Single-scar. 'Were there bandages?'

'Yes.'

'Well, then.'

'Well, then, *what*?'

Single-scar sighed.

'You don't get bandages with typhoid, do you?'

'No, I suppose not.'

'Nor with any other fever. Smallpox or something.'

'Well, no.'

'So what do you get them with?'

'Wounds, I suppose. Wounds of some sort.'

'There you are, then!'

'You're telling me that all those people there have been wounded?'

'Well, they don't put the bandages on for nothing, do they?'

'How did they get wounded?'

Single-scar looked at him suspiciously.

'I thought you knew that. I thought that maybe that was why you was here.'

'Just tell me,' said Dmitri.

Double-scar could wait no longer.

'I was there, see,' he said. 'I saw it all. In fact, they would have bloody got me, only when I saw them loading the rifles I thought, bloody hell, that's not for practice, and down I flops. I was away to the side anyway, so when it starts, away I rolls, and down a little bank and into some bushes and there I bloody stays until it's finished. But I saw it, I saw it all.'

'Let's get this straight,' said Dmitri, things clicking at last: 'when did this happen? On the journey here?'

'Yes. We were in them woods about two days' walk from Tiumen. I don't know how it was, whether somebody was trying to get away or something. But I don't think it was that. They were standing there arguing and then the guards started unshipping their guns, and then I thought, bloody hell, this is getting serious. So down I flops.'

'They opened fire?'

'They opened and then they went on. They went on till they were all down. Every bloody one!'

'I don't call that right,' said Single-scar. 'You don't need to do it to everyone, do you? One or two would do. I mean, that's what you would expect. But to do it to them all, that's not right, is it? I mean, that's a bloody massacre!'

'They went on till they was all down,' said Double-scar. 'They was all lying there. There was smoke all over the clearing, drifting, like a great cloud. I just lay there. I was in no hurry to move, I can tell you. Well, then they begins to go round, and I thought, Jesus! They're going to finish them off! But they just sort of prodded them with their guns and stood around looking at each other, as if they didn't know what to do next. Well, then an officer comes, and he says Jesus! You stupid bastards! and he looks at the sergeant and says "What are we going to do?" And the sergeant says: "Let's put them on the carts. They're sick, aren't they? Let's put them on the carts."

'So someone goes off to fetch the carts. It takes an age. And all the time they're lying there, and I'm lying there – I'm not going to bloody move, I can tell you. Well, then the carts start coming and they begin to load them on. And the drivers, they're ordinary muzhiks, you know, they don't like it, and they say: "Aren't you going to do anything for them?"

'Well, then they go and fetch the doctor and he gets busy and after a while he says, "Christ, I can't do it all myself, can I? Get someone to go with them on the carts and look after them till we get to Tiumen." But the bit I don't like is them groaning. I didn't notice it at first. I'd still got the bangs in my ears and I was a bit stupid from it all. But then when they started putting them on the carts, and while they were still lying there, and afterwards when they'd loaded them and they were beginning to move away, I suddenly noticed it. The groaning. Christ, it was going on and on.'

'That's not right, is it?' said Single-scar. 'I mean, that's not right.'

'No, it's not right,' said Dmitri.

'Well, I don't know how many was killed. But with all them in the ward, all wounded, it stands to reason some of them must have been killed, doesn't it? Well, I don't know how many that was or what happened to them. They put them all on the carts. I just lay there till they was all gone and then I hopped out quick, I can tell you.'

'They took them straight to the infirmary,' said Single-scar. 'They didn't take them to the prison, like they normally do.'

'They wanted to hush it up, see,' said Double-scar. 'They wanted to hush it up. But I don't reckon you can hush up a thing like that, can you? Someone will know something and some time it's going to get out.'

'Yes, but you can hush it up for long enough,' said Single-scar. 'We thought they was going to get away with it. And then you came. We thought that someone back in St Petersburg had got wind of it and sent you. I mean, this cock-and-bull story about a girl! And then you didn't exactly behave like, well, what you'd normally expect from a judge. So we thought – '

'You didn't seem to be getting anywhere,' said Double-scar. 'So we thought maybe you needed a bit of help.'

'Yes, well, I do,' said Dmitri, brain whirling.

'The fact is, we wanted to do something and we didn't know how to set about it. "You need a bloody lawyer for that," said Ivan. Well, I wasn't so sure. I've seen a few lawyers in my time. I reckoned they wouldn't be too keen to involve themselves in something like this. And then, how do you get hold of one? The right sort of one, I mean? And then you came along.'

'We'll pay. That's what you've got to do with lawyers, isn't it? I mean, we'd want to do this on the right basis. Do it properly. We'll all club together and pay a bit into the Artel – I mean, it'll be cigarettes and such, but you don't need to worry about that. By the time it gets to you, it'll be real money.'

'Look, you don't need – ' began Dmitri.

'No, no. We want to do it properly. Get a good lawyer, says Ivan. Well, I don't know if you're a good lawyer, you look a bit young to me, but you're the only one around so I reckon you'll have to do. How about it, then?'

'It's a deal,' said Dmitri.

But first there were a few things, a few hundred things, to be worked out. Dazed, Dmitri went back to his room and tried to make sense of all the things that had happened to him in the last few days.

What they had said seemed incredible. But then, quite a lot of the things that had happened to him recently were incredible. Was it credible, for instance, that he, Dmitri Kameron, Examining Magistrate at the Court House at Kursk, should creep like a thief through the night and spy through a hole in the wall of a prison infirmary? Was it credible that he should have to break into prison in order to conduct his inquiries? Was the subject of his inquiries itself credible – a girl from a well-to-do family in the provinces sent into exile in Siberia apparently by accident? And was it credible that when at last, after considerable difficulties, she had been located, she would have refused to return home?

Yet he had seen the bandages himself. All right, that was not enough in itself to establish the truth of the Scarfaces' assertions; there might simply have been a dreadful accident, a collision of carts, perhaps, or even some frightful explosion, which had resulted in injuries which had needed to be bandaged. It was something he would need to find independent evidence for. But one thing was certain, and he didn't need independent evidence of that: the authorities were trying to hush up something.

Was that, however, any concern of his? Well, yes, it was, for in some way or other Anna Semeonova had got caught up in the business and the effort to hush things up had extended to her. It could even be, although at the moment he couldn't quite see how, that whatever they were trying to keep quiet was bound up in some way with Anna Semeonova's refusal to be repatriated.

So, yes, it was a concern of his, a proper subject for investigation. And since for the moment, for the life of him, he couldn't see any way of making further progress on the Anna Semeonova affair, he would, yes, he would, give it some attention.

The first thing to do was to establish what had happened. Something had happened, there was no doubt about that, for afterwards the hospital carts, and the ward, had been full, so full that extra nursing help had had to be called in. Had shots been fired? That ought to be possible to establish. There must, after all, have been plenty of witnesses.

Here, however, Dmitri paused. Witnesses, there might be; but would he be able to get anything from them? The guards wouldn't talk, they would be afraid of incriminating themselves, and they would have been ordered not to say anything, anyway. The victims were in the infirmary and at the moment he could not get access to them. The drivers of the hospital carts? Perhaps, but if they were anything like your average muzhik, centuries of experience would have taught them to lie low and say nothing.

Where, then, to start? The place itself? If shots had been fired, there should be some evidence of it. Although people would not talk, the place might.

So late in the spring, the snow that had fallen the night before had not stayed. Here and there beneath the trees there were white patches, but they were melting fast. What was left was mud, which flew up in a steady spray behind the wheels of the *tarantas* and was kicked up to the occasional disconcertment of the passenger by the hooves of the horses in front.

Dmitri had been obliged to travel by *tarantas* because at this time of year there was no other vehicle available. The *tarantas* was a large, heavy, four-wheeled wagon with a boat-shaped body resting on two long poles which ran fore and aft connecting the front axle with the rear axle and serving to some extent as springs. The driver sat sideways on the edge of the carriage in front of the passenger and drove three horses harnessed abreast.

Once the horses had got up speed they could maintain about six miles an hour. At that rate it would take three hours to get to the nearest post station and the place where the massacre had occurred was, according to the Artel, two miles beyond that. He should be able to manage the whole journey, there and back, within the day.

The horse express service, which had supplied the *tarantas*, was a private company and he had had no difficulty in hiring transport. At this time of year there wasn't much demand for its services and the company's agent at Tiumen had been only too glad to supply Dmitri with horses and driver. The driver, possibly, had been less keen, but then he had not been consulted.

'Muddy,' said Dmitri conversationally, once they had got into the forest.

'More comfortable,' said the driver.

'Comfortable?' said Dmitri, thrown continuously from one side of the vehicle to the other by its heavy jolting.

'Softer ground,' said the driver. 'You should come in the summer. Or the winter,' he added.

'Thanks,' said Dmitri. 'I won't.'

He had been quite looking forward to escaping from the confines of the prison for the day. Dmitri was not one for the open air, but was beginning to feel oppressed by the closedness of the prison. He seemed to have spent the whole of his time lately behind walls. Something of the same feeling of confinement persisted, however, in the forest. The trees were thick and dark and the sky seemed to have disappeared. There was only the track leading through the wood, a great, broad thoroughfare torn up by hooves and wheels and so pounded by the many feet that had passed that it had dropped a foot or two below the level of the surrounding woodland. At least you couldn't miss it.

By the time they reached the post station, Dmitri felt much pounded too. He was hardly able to descend to the ground.

'A bowl of soup for the Barin?' suggested the station keeper.

It was brought by a sturdy girl who seemed disposed to chat.

'What's this, Your Honour?' she said. 'Coming back this way this afternoon? You won't have time to get anywhere.'

'I'm not going far.'

'Where are you going, then? There's nothing between here and Derevitsa.'

'I just want to look at a place a couple of miles further on.'

'Oh,' she said. 'Why's that?'

'Something happened there a couple of weeks ago.'

'Yes,' she said. 'We saw the carts.'

'Varya!' called the station keeper.

The girl took no notice.

'There was blood all over the carts,' she said. 'It was dripping down.'

'Did you hear anything? Earlier?'

'Yes,' she said. 'I heard something.'

The station keeper appeared.

'Varya,' he said, 'you'd best come when I call. Otherwise there'll be trouble.'

'I'm coming, aren't I?'

The girl flounced out.

'The Barin's horses are ready,' said the station keeper. He stood waiting for Dmitri. Dmitri rose from the table and went out into the yard. The driver was already in his place. Dmitri looked up at him.

'It's a cold day,' he said to the station keeper. 'Have a jug of vodka waiting for us when we get back.'

He climbed into the carriage. It didn't take them long to cover the couple of miles. Dmitri had been told what to look for and when they got there he ordered the driver to stop.

The track widened out at that point into a small clearing. Here and there were the ashes of past fires. It was an occasional stopping place for the convoy.

Dmitri climbed down and began to circle the clearing. Near one edge of it he found what he wanted. Lying half-buried in the mud were a number of spent cartridge cases. He counted over sixty of them.

There were a few torn pieces of cloth, so muddy that he could not see if they were stained. However, he picked them up and put them in his pocket, along with some of the cartridge cases.

He found some twigs and stones and tried to see if any of them were discoloured, but it was very hard to tell among the mud and the gravel weathering. There were no stones on the ground. The universal mud had covered everything.

He stood for a moment sketching the spot. Then he turned and climbed back into the *tarantas*.

Back at the post station fresh horses, and a jug of vodka, were waiting. He gave the vodka to the driver and ordered tea for himself. The girl brought it.

He took out one of the cartridge cases and laid it on the table.

'It's not just hunters who have guns,' said the girl.

Dmitri, unusually, felt the need to take legal advice. He had never found himself in that position at Kursk, reasoning, probably correctly, that he knew more about the law than any of the other lawyers there. Peter Ivanovich knew more about procedural tripwires, but of larger issues he knew nothing. Indeed, it was to that that he owed his advancement. At university, certainly in his first term, Dmitri had been prepared to accept that the Professor of Law knew more than he did, but that point soon passed. Ever since then he had felt able to rely on his own judgement. Now, suddenly, he found himself in need of advice.

He could have done with a few professors here. If he had been at Kursk he might even have gone up to St Petersburg to have a word with the Faculty; but Tiumen was even further from civilization than Kursk and there was no Faculty of Law within a million miles.

All there was was – well, there was Grigori. Grigori was the exact opposite of Peter Ivanovich. Of procedural tripwires he knew nothing, which was probably why he was going to Siberia. On larger issues, though … But what about the issues in between? It was there that Dmitri felt he needed help. On larger issues, Dmitri felt he could speculate with the best. It was where the larger issues became real that he felt he could do with some help.

He feared that Grigori was not likely to be of much use there. Nevertheless, he was at hand and Dmitri, strangely, was inclined to trust his judgement. He went down to the yard.

He found Grigori sitting on the ground reading and sat down beside him.

'What exactly', he said, 'are the powers of an Examining Magistrate in Siberia?'

'What they are in Kursk, so far as ordinary people are concerned, that is.'

'What about politicals?'

'Well, of course, there is no specific reference to political exiles as such in the Code of Surveillance.'

'No reference?'

'The relevant sentence is: "Persons prejudicial to public tranquillity …"'

'You, for instance?'

Grigori beamed.

'Me, for instance "… may be assigned by administrative process to definite places of residence".'

'Prison, for example?'

'Exactly. The relevant phrase, though, is "administrative process". It means that if a prisoner wishes to initiate any form of legal action – an appeal, for instance – he or she cannot have recourse to the courts. The only authority is the administrative one. That, I am afraid, applies to you, too. You can exercise your powers only with the consent of the appropriate administrative authority, that is, the Ministry of the Interior.'

'So that if I wished to gain access to particular prisoners or a particular part of the prison, the Governor would be within his rights to deny it me?'

'You could go over his head. But it would have to be to the Ministry.'

'And what if there is a possible question of illegal action by the Governor himself? Or by the Administration?'

'You would have to be sure that it *was* illegal. If it arises in the course of his or its duties then the only question would be whether reasonable process had been followed.'

'It would be an internal matter?'

'That's right.'

'Is there any way in which I could make it an external matter?'

'You could call for a Public Inquiry.'

'But only call for it? I couldn't somehow … bring it about?'

'Not by any legal means, no.'

Grigori was not the only person that Dmitri wanted to see. Konstantin, the doctor, was another. He, too, was in the yard, talking to some other prisoners.

'Found your girlfriend yet?' he said to Dmitri with a smile.

'Not yet.'

After a while he was able to take the doctor aside.

'Actually, I have found her. She's over there in the infirmary. In a special ward.'

'Special ward? There is one, is there? I thought there was.'

'You didn't get a chance to look inside it?'

'No. They kept us to the main wards.'

'You've no idea what the patients there were treated for?'

'No, not at all, I'm afraid. You're worried that it might be infectious? That your girlfriend could – '

'No, no. It's not that. I think the patients in that ward might all be suffering from gunshot wounds.'

'Gunshot wounds!'

'I'd like to find out. Is there any way that you could help me?'

Konstantin thought.

'Evidence of treatment, you mean?' He shook his head. 'As I said, they kept us pretty separate. It was only the one time that I saw that girl. She'd come in for something. I'm trying to think what it was. Something fairly ordinary. Bandages?'

'There were other nursing orderlies, presumably – the normal ones, I mean. Do they ever come over here?'

'To the main prison? I don't think so.'

'What about food, supplies, equipment? Does that get taken straight there or does someone come over here to get it?'

'It gets taken over. I'm pretty sure the nursing orderlies stay over there.'

'Nevertheless, we could probably get a message in. Is there someone over there who might know? Whom you could ask?'

Konstantin tried to think.

'There's the senior orderly, Pavel Gregorovich. He might know.'

'Would he be prepared to say? If you asked him?'

'He might.'

Dmitri noted the name.

'But, listen,' said Konstantin worriedly, 'if it's gunshot wounds … There ought to be doctors there.'

'There are. The Prison Service ones.'

He looked at Konstantin.

'*Only* the Prison Service ones.'

'I see.'

'I need independent evidence.'

'I don't think there's anything I can do. But if there is …' He brightened. 'Perhaps they'll send for me again. If they do, I promise you I'll find a way of getting a look at that ward. I might even', he said, elated, 'have a word with that girlfriend of yours! What did you say her name was?'

'Shumin,' said Dmitri. 'But that's not – '

'Shumin?' said a harsh, familiar voice, with sudden interest. 'Shumin?'

It was Dmitri's unpleasant adversary of the party, Gasparov, who had been with the group that Konstantin had been talking to and who had overheard the last remark.

'Shumin?' he said. 'Who is this Shumin?'

'Dmitri's girlfriend. He's been looking for her.'

'Ah, so?'

Gasparov gave Dmitri a puzzled look.

'But why were you not with her on the convoy?'

'Dmitri came later,' said Konstantin.

'Ah, a later detachment?'

'Dmitri's been trying to track her down. She's not in the ordinary prison, you see. Nor in the cells.'

'No,' said Gasparov. 'That is correct.'

'He thinks she's in the infirmary.'

'Of course! That is where she would be! She has been – hurt?'

At the time, Dmitri did not notice it. He didn't want to talk about Anna Semeonova with anyone like Gasparov. In fact, he didn't want to talk to Gasparov at all.

'Just helping,' he said. 'With the nursing.'

'Ah! But – '

However Dmitri definitely didn't want to talk to Gasparov and moved determinedly away.

Upstairs in his room, lying on the bed, Dmitri had much to think about. Anna Semeonova, for a start. He had at last found her. But Anna Semeonova dwindled into insignificance when compared with what else he had found out; or thought he had found out. There had been some sort of incident on the convoy's way out. An ugly incident. Even if no one had been killed – and, surely, someone must have been – people, many people, had been wounded. The cries, the carts, the blood, sixty spent cartridge cases – sixty! That was no hunting party. No, massacre was what the Scarfaces had called it, and massacre was what it was.

And yet it had all been hushed up! Or would have been if ... Still could be, he told himself. Abstract him from the scene and what would remain? Prisoners distributed through all the camps in Siberia. Who in Vladivostok would bother to ask how they had acquired their wounds? Compromised prison guards in whose interest it was to say nothing. Doctors who had learned to treat patients without inquiring too closely into the nature of their ailments. An Administration which answered only to those who preferred not to know about the messy detail of what went on in the remote tundra, a messiness which anyway they would probably regard as necessary.

Out here, people could disappear without leaving a gap. There wouldn't even be a gap in the records. They could disappear as suddenly and completely as – as, well, Anna Semeonova might have done.

If it had not been for the accident of his pursuing Anna Semeonova, none of this would have come out. But now it was going to come out. Oh, yes, it definitely was.

But …

Legal recourse, so far as he could see, there was none. The Prison Administration was a law unto itself, the Ministry of the Interior even more so. Public Inquiry it would have to be. Grigori was right.

On the say-so of a junior Examining Magistrate? Dmitri thought he was important, but not that important. The public would have to be moved. That would not be easy with the strict censorship of the press, and with the Ministry of the Interior doing the censoring. They would excise any reference to an incident such as this. He would have to gain the ear of someone important in St Petersburg. That would not be easy, either. Dmitri was not so naive as not to know that anyone like that would be a lot more likely to listen to the Ministry of the Interior than they were to him.

Evidence; he would need evidence. Well, evidence of a sort there was: the cartridge cases, for instance. But they carried weight only in relation to his own testimony, as to the circumstance in which he had found them, for example; and how much weight would the voice of a junior Examining Magistrate carry?

He would need more: the voices of other people beside himself.

Yet here, too, there were difficulties. Whose voices? Prisoners' voices? They would be discounted. The girl at the post station in the forest? Her father or her boss would probably beat her into saying nothing anyway, but even if she did, how much weight would an ordinary peasant girl carry? Konstantin? A doctor, after all. Suppose he could be got in some way to examine the patients in the special ward? But Konstantin was a prisoner, too. His was another of the discounted voices.

He needed someone who could not be discounted, whose voice would have to be heard. And then suddenly he had it. Anna Semeonova! Anna Semeonova, whose voice would have to be heard because she was the daughter of a well-to-do family in the provinces, because her disappearance was a *cause célèbre* at Kursk; and because it was the Administration's bungling that had sent her into Siberia! Anna Semeonova, who had travelled on the bloody carts, who had nursed the wounded in the infirmary at Tiumen, and who might well have been taken to the scene of the massacre immediately afterwards!

Anna Semeonova it would have to be; but would she do it?

11

'I need to see Anna Semeonova again,' he said to Methodosius. 'Can you speak to the Artel?'

'Anna Semeonova?'

'Shumin. Tell them it's connected with the other business. It's very important.'

The next day Methodosius came up to him in the yard.

'They say they have no one of that name over there.'

'But that's ridiculous! I spoke to her. The Artel arranged it.'

'Well that's what the women say. And without them, the Artel can't do anything.'

Then Dmitri remembered.

'She's calling herself something else. Try Marya Serafimovna.'

'But – ' said Timofei.

Methodosius went away. Some time later he returned.

'It's all right now,' he said. 'They've fixed it for tomorrow night.'

'What are they playing at?' said Dmitri.

Methodosius shrugged.

'I don't know,' he said. 'All I know is, if you want to see Shumin, you can't. If you want to see Serafimovna, you can.'

'But – ' said Timofei.

'What's the trouble?'

'You don't want to see Marya. You want to see – well, this other girl.'

'Yes, but she's calling herself Serafimovna.'

'But she can't! Serafimovna is someone *else*. I know her!'

'You do?'

'She comes from our village. Of course I know her! She's been a neighbour of mine for fifteen years. What's this girl doing calling herself by her name?'

'Well I don't know. But that's what she told me. "I'm not Anna Semeonova any more," she said. "Nor Shumin either. I'm Marya Serafimovna now."'

'But that *can't* be right!'

Dmitri looked at Methodosius.

'That may be,' said Methodosius. 'You may be right, old fellow. But if you're right, then all the women over there are wrong. For they're going along with her!'

'But – ' said Timofei, then collapsed into bewilderment.

Dmitri was bewildered too; more than bewildered, irritated. What was the girl playing at? She seemed to change names as easily as other people changed clothes. She was just mucking about. But this was no time for messing around, there were serious things to be done. He really must speak to her.

But in order to speak to her, he would have to play along with her, humour her. Well, if that's what she insisted on, that's what he would have to do. Still, he really couldn't see the point –

There must be some point.

'This Marya Serafimovna,' he said to Timofei; 'she comes from your village?'

'Yes.'

'She's a Milk-Drinker, then?'

'We're all Milk-Drinkers in our village.'

'Was she with you on the convoy?'

'Yes. She was taken with us. It was all wrong. She had just had a child. She wasn't strong enough yet. I tried to get her a place on the carts.'

'But she had to walk with you? Was she one of the Milk-Drinkers they called away to work on the hospital carts?'

'Yes. And I said: "You go, Marya. Get yourself a ride. You'll never make it, otherwise." So off she went.'

Then she had been on the hospital carts. And presumably she'd gone to the infirmary with the others. But why had they exchanged names, Dmitri wondered? In fact, though, they hadn't exchanged names. Anna Semeonova had simply taken hers. But what had happened to the Milk-Drinker?

He saw Gasparov coming towards him. Gasparov was the last person he wanted to talk to just at the moment and he tried to move away. Gasparov, however, intercepted him.

'Please!' he said. 'There is something we must discuss.'

Dmitri, however, had gone off discussion.

'Yes?' he said unwillingly.

'Please! It is important.' He paused. 'What exactly is the nature of your interest in Shumin?'

'My interest in Shumin?' said Dmitri, surprised.

'Yes. The doctor spoke of her as your girlfriend. That I cannot believe.'

'Well, no …'

'Ah, no?' said Gasparov, pleased. 'But what, then, is the nature of your interest in her?'

Dmitri hesitated. There was on the face of it no reason why he shouldn't tell Gasparov, but something held him back.

'You are cautious,' said Gasparov approvingly. 'Well, that is wise. People like us need to be cautious.'

People like us? What *was* he talking about? Then he realized. Gasparov, having seen him in the cell with the politicals, thought he was a political too.

'I, too, am interested in Shumin,' Gasparov pronounced.

'Yes?'

'We must work together.'

'Ye-es?' said Dmitri more doubtfully.

Gasparov smiled.

'Still cautious? Well, we do not know each other. But it is surely not a coincidence that we are both … interested in Shumin. Perhaps your interest is the same as mine.'

He seemed to be waiting.

Dmitri couldn't think what to say. How could their interest be the same? Was the fellow a police agent or something?

'Perhaps,' he temporized.

Gasparov seemed disappointed. He shrugged.

'Well, let us go our separate ways, then. Perhaps after … But, my friend, perhaps this I should say, in case you have to act alone. Have you known her long?'

'Not very, no.'

'Nor I. I have known her long enough, though, to have found out that she is unreliable.'

'Unreliable?'

'And that way, my friend, for people like us, danger lies. But perhaps you know that already. Perhaps others have found that out. And perhaps that is why you have come.'

He smiled significantly and then moved away. Dmitri was totally mystified.

The next night things proceeded as before. Shortly after midnight he descended into the yard, where he found the two men from the Artel waiting for him. There was no snow this time, however. The night was cloudy but every now and then the moon appeared through a break in the clouds and lit up everything alarmingly. They kept to the shadows where they could. Crossing the road, they waited for cloud. On the other side they hugged the infirmary wall.

The gate was open as before. The men went straight to the right place this time. Dmitri bent and put his face to the chink.

The ward was quite still. In the pale candlelight he could see the patients lying in their beds. Bandaged. One of them was holding an ikon clasped to his breast.

Something stirred on the other side of the wall and then he found a face close to his and felt himself brushed by a wisp of hair.

'You should not have come,' said Anna Semeonova.

'I need your help.'

'You need *my* help?' said Anna Semeonova, astonished.

'Yes. I want you to be a witness.'

'Witness?'

'They won't believe me. Not if it's me alone. And anyone else I could get, they won't believe either, because they'd be a convicted prisoner.'

'I am a convicted prisoner,' said Anna Semeonova.

'A prisoner, yes. But not convicted.'

There was a long silence.

'What do you want me to witness to?' said Anna Semeonova, a little shakily.

'You were on the convoy. They asked you to help on the carts. You saw the people who were put on them. Didn't you?'

'Yes,' said Anna Semeonova.

'They had been shot, hadn't they? They had been shot down?'

Her 'yes' was so faint that he could hardly hear it.

'They were taken to the infirmary and you have been nursing them. You know the nature of their wounds. You can testify to their having been shot.'

There was no reply.

'Well?' said Dmitri.

'I don't know,' said Anna Semeonova.

'What don't you know? You saw the people, didn't you?'

'Yes,' said the girl reluctantly. 'I saw the people.'

'Did you actually see them being lifted on to the carts?'

'Yes,' she said faintly.

'Well, then,' said Dmitri, 'that's all you have to say. That would do.'

There was no reply.

'You will do it?' said Dmitri after a while. 'You must do it!'

'I can't,' she said.

'You needn't be frightened. You will be under my protection. The Court's protection,' amplified Dmitri, feeling that she might well judge the offer of his own services, unassisted, insufficient.

'I cannot,' she said.

God, they were back to that, to her original mysterious refusal to return with him.

'You must!' he said determinedly. 'You cannot allow a dreadful thing like this to go unpunished!'

She said something that he couldn't quite catch and he asked her to repeat it. She did, but again he couldn't catch it. It sounded like 'Someone else.'

'It has to be you,' he said. 'You're the only one who would do. They won't believe anyone else, or they'll say they can't believe anybody else. They'd be able to hush it up.'

He thought he heard a faint sob.

'You don't want that, do you?'

'No.'

'Then you've got to help. It's got to be you. No one else will do.'

'I can't,' she said again, shakily.

'Why can't you?'

'I just can't!'

'Why can't you? You must tell me. You can't let those people die and do nothing!'

He had to wait for so long that he thought for a moment she'd gone away.

'I was there,' she said.

'Well, then – '

'No, no, you don't understand. I was there. I saw it happen.'

'You saw it happen?'

'Yes.'

'Saw the actual shooting?'

'Yes.'

Now the silence was Dmitri's.

'They pressed forward,' she said, so quietly that Dmitri could hardly hear, 'shouting. And the guards were shouting back. And then someone – the sergeant, I think – shouted, "Stand back, or I'll fire!" And they still pressed forward. And then the guards began shooting, and they went on and on, until everyone was lying there, and there was smoke everywhere, and noise …'

Her voice died away. Dmitri waited a moment, needed to wait for a moment, and then said gently:

'Well, that is what you must say. You must say it, because something like this cannot be allowed to happen and nothing be done about it. I know it is distressing – '

'It is not that,' she said quickly. 'Not just that.'

'No?'

'No. You see … I caused it. I was to blame.'

'Oh, come – '

'No, I was to blame. I *am* to blame. I caused it, and – ' so faint that he could hardly hear – 'I did it deliberately.'

'Come,' said Dmitri, 'I am sure that whatever you did, you didn't do it deliberately, intending innocent people to be shot down – '

'No, no,' she said. 'Not that! I didn't think – I didn't think for one moment – and then when it started happening I tried to run forward and explain, but something, or someone, hit me, and I fell, and when I looked up it was all happening, and I couldn't believe it, and I just lay there stunned, no, not stunned, not unconscious, but – I was in a daze, I couldn't – '

'Look,' said Dmitri, 'you really must not blame yourself.'

'No,' she said, 'that is exactly what I must do. Because without me, it wouldn't have happened.'

'Perhaps', said Dmitri, 'you had better tell me. Tell me everything.'

One of the men from the Artel plucked at his sleeve. Dmitri shook his head determinedly. The man's hand fell away.

Anna Semeonova didn't say anything for a while. Then she caught her breath and began resolutely.

'It goes back a long way. To Kursk.'

'The Court House?' said Dmitri.

'Even before. I had got to know Marfa Shumin. I admired her. She seemed to be everything I was not. Brave, and good, and purposeful. She had a purpose in life and I had none. I wanted to help other people but I couldn't see – and somehow she could. I admired her, I admired her very much. And then when she got taken away by the police, a person like that! I wrote to her; I said, was there anything I could do, and she wrote back and said, no, there wasn't, that they would send her to Siberia and that was that. It seemed all wrong to me, it *was* all wrong. I went to the Court House that day wanting to help but not really knowing what I could do – '

'The day we met at the Court House?' said Dmitri.

'Yes. I wanted to see her. I had some vague notion about changing places with her, about sacrificing myself. Well, we went out into the yard, didn't we, and then I sent you away. And then there was a chance and – well, I took it', said Anna Semeonova simply.

'Had you arranged it beforehand?'

'No, no. And when I spoke to Marfa, she couldn't believe it, she just stood there, and I pushed her out of the way, and then I saw that boy looking at me, so I climbed up into the cart – '

'And went to Siberia in her place.'

'Yes.'

'It was a stupid thing to do.'

'Yes, I know that now.'

'But then why,' said Dmitri, 'why did you refuse to come back to Kursk with me?'

'Because of what happened. That dreadful ... that dreadful thing in the forest.'

'Why should that stop you?'

'Because I was to blame.'

'How could you be to blame?'

Another long silence. Then she started again, shaky but determined.

'There was a man in the convoy,' she said. 'He thought I was Shumin. And I played along, because I *was* Shumin. Or, at least, I wanted to be. But he began to talk to me about all kinds of terrible things, as if I was sure to be interested in such things and – and would want to do them. But I couldn't believe that Marfa ... I still don't. But she was known to him as a – as a revolutionary, and he thought she *would* be interested and would want to – to help him.'

'How could she help him? If he was going to Siberia?'

'The Tsar's regime was there, too, he said, and we could strike a blow there as well as we could anywhere else. And I listened, I just listened, I had no intention ... But he went on talking and gradually it became clear he wanted my help. He said it was best if it was a woman. It would be easier to get people involved, men involved especially. He said that criminals were like that, he said it with a sort of sneer on his face, that they were stupid and would be more likely to get involved if it was a woman. It was important to get men involved because then there would be more chance of it getting out of hand. It had to be big, you see, big enough for people to notice, people back in Russia. It would show people what the Tsar's regime was like, was really like. It would strike a great blow at it, and, and ...'

Anna Semeonova stopped.

'And?' prompted Dmitri.

'I wanted to strike a blow,' she whispered.

'He had persuaded you?'

'A bit. It was more, though, that I asked myself what Marfa Shumin would do, and I thought that perhaps, yes, she *would* want to strike a blow, and I thought that if she would have done it then surely I ought to …'

'What exactly did he ask you to do?'

'I had to talk to people on the march and pretend that the guards had attacked me.'

'But surely – ' began Dmitri.

'Not in that way,' she said. 'They don't attack you in that way. They hit you, but on the whole they don't hit you very much, it's more the men. It's like the criminals,' she said. 'They don't attack you either. It's odd, isn't it?'

'So you did talk to people?'

'Yes. I said it had happened at the last stop. I told some of the women and they spread it, and there were men there and they became angry. I don't know quite how it came to flare up, but then suddenly …'

'And what about this man, then? What happened to him?'

'I don't know. He wasn't in the infirmary. Perhaps – perhaps he was one of the dead.'

'If anyone is to blame,' said Dmitri, 'it is him and not you.'

'He is certainly to blame,' said Anna Semeonova. 'But so am I.'

'I don't think – '

'I should have foreseen it. I thought it would just end in shouts and blows. I didn't think for one moment … But, of course, I should have thought. I was too innocent,' said Anna Semeonova. 'What I now know is that innocence is no excuse.'

'And so,' said Dmitri, 'you have set out to punish yourself? By condemning yourself to Siberia?'

'It's appropriate, isn't it?'

'No,' said Dmitri. 'It's not appropriate.'

But Anna Semeonova would not be moved.

'Listen, mate,' said one of the men from the Artel, 'we can't stay here all night.'

'Shut up!' said Dmitri. 'I'm thinking.'

'He's thinking,' said one Artel man to the other.

'Well, I'm thinking, too,' said the other Artel man. 'I'm thinking we should bloody well get out of this.'

'Get out of it if you want!' said Dmitri.

'Are you coming, then?'

'No.'

The men looked at each other.

'Here,' said one, 'you've got to come. Otherwise the Artel will have our balls.'

'I'm not coming,' said Dmitri.

'You must go,' said Anna Semeonova.

'There's something I don't understand,' said Dmitri. 'Why have you changed places with Marya Serafimovna?'

'Not changed,' said Anna Semeonova. 'I've just taken her place, that's all.'

'How could that be?'

'She died,' said Anna Semeonova. 'She was very weak, poor thing. I talked about it with the Milk-Drinkers. They suggested it, in fact.'

'I don't understand.'

'People die here all the time,' said Anna Semeonova. 'They don't inquire too closely about the bodies. A body passed out. Marya Serafimovna stays. That's all.'

'But why?' asked Dmitri.

'I don't want to be Shumin. Not any more. And, besides ...'

'Yes?'

'I want to be Marya Serafimovna.'

'I must ask you again: Why?'

She hesitated.

'Mr Kameron – ' Dmitri was oddly pleased at this use of his name – 'do you know anything about the Milk-Drinkers?'

'Well …'

'They're good people. They're about the only good people I've met. I didn't meet many good people at Kursk. Vera Samsonova, perhaps, but she's not exactly good, not in the way the Milk-Drinkers are. There's something special about them. Have you noticed, Mr Kameron? They're against shooting. They're against all violence, whether it's the stupid, mindless violence of the criminals or the kind of violence that the Government uses all the time. Well, I'm not a good person, Mr Kameron, but that will do for me. I've decided to become a Milk-Drinker.'

'Look, mate,' said the man from the Artel.

'Shut up!' said Dmitri.

'He's thinking,' said the other man.

'He's not thinking enough,' said the first man. 'It's time we got out of here.'

'You've got to come back with me,' said Dmitri. 'If you don't come back with me I can't do anything!'

'I'm sorry,' said Anna Semeonova.

'I need you as a witness. You saw it all. You can't just step aside. You must stand up and testify.'

'Testify?' said Anna Semeonova.

'Look, mate,' pleaded the man from the Artel 'if we don't go now – '

'Yes, go!' said Anna Semeonova. 'I must think.'

'Jesus!' said the man from the Artel. 'Not another one!'

Dmitri felt he had to tell Timofei about Marya Serafimovna. Timofei nodded his head in acceptance.

'The Lord gives,' he said softly, 'and the Lord takes away.'

For Dmitri, there was too much quiescence in it. Why should the Lord take away? He, Dmitri, would have protested.

'Marya Serafimovna I can understand,' he said. 'Just. She was sick and ill. You can argue it would have happened anyway. But the others, the ones in the forest – no, I don't think that's to be accepted.'

'No,' agreed Timofei. 'Not without doing anything.'

'I'll do what I can,' said Dmitri. 'I'm afraid, though, that no one's going to listen much to a junior Examining Magistrate.'

'Not even a Magistrate?' said Timofei, opening his eyes in surprise.

'I would have to produce evidence that they couldn't brush away. More to the point, I want to produce some*one* they can't brush away.'

'It's a pity she's not your sweetheart,' said Timofei regretfully. 'Then she would do what you asked.'

Dmitri, surprisingly, found himself thinking not of Anna Semeonova but of Vera Samsonova.

'No,' he said. 'I don't think it's quite like that.'

'All the same,' said Timofei, 'she will come back with you.'

'I doubt it,' said Dmitri despondently.

'She will. She has to, you see. If she's a Milk-Drinker. You said she had become a Milk-Drinker?'

'Yes, but …'

'A Milk-Drinker', said Timofei, 'has to bear witness.'

It wasn't quite the same thing, though, thought Dmitri. He would have liked to have had another talk with Anna Semeonova, another go at persuading her. Instead, he saw Gasparov coming towards him.

'Still cautious?' asked Gasparov.

Dmitri did not know what to make of the man's strange confidences.

'Yes,' he said shortly.

'A pity. We could have worked together.'

'I doubt it.'

Gasparov, however, was not to be put off.

'You're not here by accident, are you?' he said. 'Someone sent you.'

'Well, yes.'

Dmitri saw no reason why he shouldn't admit it.

'I thought so!' said Gasparov triumphantly. 'And then, when I heard that you were looking for Shumin, I thought … well, I thought that perhaps our interests might coincide. You see, on the way here I was able to strike a blow – '

'Strike a blow?'

'Yes. Even in prison, my friend, it is possible to work for the cause.'

'I see.'

Gasparov looked at him.

'You have, perhaps, heard?'

'Something.'

Gasparov seemed disappointed.

'It is important that it gets out.'

'Oh, I think it will,' said Dmitri. 'I think it will.'

'You do?' said Gasparov, pleased.

'Tell me,' said Dmitri, 'have you, too, been sent?'

'Oh, no,' said Gasparov. 'I was caught in the ordinary way. But even in prison the struggle must go on. So when I saw my chance, I took it. And I shall take it', he said, 'again and again. But for that I must remain undetected. That is why, my friend, I am interested in you; and your interest in Shumin.'

'I'm afraid I still don't see the reason for your interest.'

'I used Shumin. I thought she was committed. But she turned out to be unreliable. The question I have been putting to myself is this: If she was unreliable once, might not she be unreliable again? Could she be counted on to keep silent? The answer, I think, is no. And that is why I am interested in you and your mission. It occurred to me that other people might have found her unreliable, too; and that that may be why you have been sent. Am I correct?'

'Not entirely,' said Dmitri.

'Our interests are not the same?'

'Not quite. I am a lawyer, Mr Gasparov. Examining Magistrate to the Court at Kursk.'

But of what use was that in the present situation? He could hardly go to the Governor and say: 'I have arrested this man'. First, because Gasparov was already a convict and therefore not under his jurisdiction, and, secondly, because that would involve telling the Governor what he knew about the incident in the forest, and he didn't want to do that until he was well clear of Siberia and back in Russia proper where someone could keep an eye on him and shout if he suddenly went missing.

And not just him; Anna Semeonova, too. It all hung on her. She was the key witness, a fact which the Governor would know as well as he did. Could he be relied on to produce her?

It would be all too easy not to. By her constant tricks with her identity, Anna Semeonova might well have played into the Governor's hands. Anna Semeonova? Lost, Your Honour, certainly; but not here in Tiumen. Back at Kursk. No evidence whatever that she ever left Kursk. Shumin? Ah, well, a different matter; she did arrive at Tiumen but then was transferred to the infirmary. Died, sadly, shortly after transfer. Body could be produced, but does Your Honour really …? Marya Serafimovna? A Milk-Drinker? Posted on in the normal way. Now at a camp over Vladivostok way. Could be found, certainly, but it would take some time …

By which time Anna Semeonova would probably be dead. No Anna Semeonova, no witness; no witness, no trial or public inquiry. Gasparov would no doubt get his just deserts; but would the Governor?

Anna Semeonova had to come back to Kursk with him. Somehow he had to persuade her. And Gasparov could wait.

The next day someone came up to him in the yard and put a slip of paper in his hands. It was from Anna Semeonova. It said:

I am willing to testify.

Dmitri and Methodosius went to see the Artel.

'You want us to get her out?'

Dmitri nodded.

'I need her out and back in Kursk.'

Single-scar was doubtful.

'Out, I daresay we could manage. Back in Kursk, though …'

'Russia would do. So long as she's out of Siberia.'

Single-scar looked at him.

'It's not just her, though, is it? It's you as well. You'll want to be with her. And you couldn't take her on the pony express. They'd have you in no time.'

Dmitri thought.

'You're right. It would have to be the two of us.'

Single-scar was unhappy.

'Out, I could manage,' he said. 'But getting you to the border – '

'Walk,' said Methodosius.

'That'd be all right for you,' said Single-scar. 'You're a Wanderer, aren't you? But they wouldn't be able to – '

'I'd go with them,' said Methodosius.

Dmitri, aware that he would soon be leaving, went to look up his political friends in the yard. Gasparov, he was glad to see, was not among them.

'I don't know that there's anything I'll be able to do for you,' he said to Grigori, 'but what I can do, I will.'

'Send some books,' said Grigori, smiling.

'I'm going to ask the Artel to try and get you over to the infirmary,' he said to Konstantin. 'Just check on the nature of the wounds. Perhaps I'll be able to call you as a witness.'

'I'll find a way,' the doctor promised.

'Oh, and don't say too much to Gasparov. He's not – well, not all that he appears to be.'

Konstantin looked at him quickly.

'No?'

'No.'

'Gasparov?' said Grigori. 'He'll be no problem. He's gone to the infirmary.'

12

'Let's get this straight,' said Single-scar. 'There's this political – '

'I told you, didn't I?' interrupted Double-scar, unable to keep quiet any longer. 'I told you!'

'Yes, you told me,' said Dmitri.

'I seen it!'

'You did.'

'He put her up to it, didn't he? That girl?'

'Yes.'

'I see her,' said Double-scar. 'I see her when it all starts. But I don't see him.'

'No, well – '

'Politicals is like that. They puts you up to it, but then when it all starts to happen, they're suddenly nowhere around. I hate politicals.'

'They leaves others to stand the racket,' said Single-scar.

'That's it! And the thing is, see, they don't do it accidental. It's all deliberate with them. They've got it worked out. That bloke, see. She wasn't the first he'd tried. He'd been going round. He'd got it all worked out, see, from the start.'

'You saw him?'

'No. But that day, that day when it all happened, people were talking about it. They were getting angry, like. There's this girl, they say. But then someone says, "It's not like that. She's been put up to it, there's this bloke been going round." But no one takes any notice. No, they say, there's something in it. Those guards are always at it. It's time it was put a stop to. And it boils over, like, and one of them goes up to a guard and says: "You bastard!" and then they starts hitting him. Well, there's always two sides to that story, and some starts hitting back. But there wasn't two sides to it when the shooting started! No. I don't blame her, though. I blames him.'

'I blame them,' said Single-scar. 'They didn't have to start shooting, did they?'

'They wouldn't have started if it hadn't been for her. And she wouldn't have got them started if it hadn't been for him. She's probably just an innocent. Like you, mate. Nothing personal intended. So I blame him.'

'The thing is,' said Dmitri, 'he's over there now.'

'We've got to do something about that,' said Single-scar.

'Why don't I go over and stick him?' suggested Double-scar.

'You leave that to me!' said Dmitri hastily.

Double-scar looked at him doubtfully.

'I don't know as you're the man for this, mate. Nothing personal intended.'

'In my way,' said Dmitri.

'Ah!' said Single-scar. 'That's just it! In his way!'

'What's so special about him?' said Double-scar, beginning to take offence.

'The thing is,' said Single-scar, 'it's not just him, that political, that we want to stick. It's them all.'

'All!' said Double-scar, daunted.

'The guards and such. All of them.'

'Jesus!' said Double-scar, impressed but worried. 'Look, I can do some of them, give me a bit of time, but – '

'That's just it,' said Single-scar. 'That's why it's got to be his way. And for that he needs her out and alive and back in Kursk.' He looked at Dmitri. 'Tonight, then?'

When Dmitri went down into the yard a little after midnight he was surprised to find not only Methodosius but Timofei.

'Well,' said Timofei, with a self-deprecating shrug, 'she's a Milk-Drinker, isn't she? Almost?'

Dmitri might have been disposed to argue, but the men from the Artel were waiting. It was the same two men as before. They slipped out of the main prison through the side gate, crept along the road for a while keeping to the shadows, and then crossed it when the moon disappeared behind a cloud. On the other side they found the steep palisade that contained the dispensary and moved softly down it until they came to the door Dmitri had used before. This time, however, they went in.

They did not have long to wait. The door opened quietly and two men came out with a girl muffled up in a long convict coat. One of the men pushed a bag into Dmitri's hands.

'You'll need that,' he said.

And then the men were gone.

Methodosius sniffed the air like a dog, lifted his eyes to the sky, and then set off unhesitatingly into the darkness.

Recounting the tale of his adventures afterwards, back in Kursk, Dmitri made light of the rigours of the journey.

'Yes,' he said, affecting nonchalance, 'it was about two hundred miles to the border. It took us just over a fortnight. But then we were walking all the time.'

'Anna Semeonova, too?' asked Sonya, round-eyed. She still could not get over the fact that her schoolfriend had somehow become a heroine.

'Of course.'

How else did Sonya think the girl had got there?

'In a way, it was easier for her than it was for me. She had, after all, walked it before,' he pointed out.

'Still …'

Sonya found it hard to come to terms with anyone walking two hundred miles, let alone someone from one of the best families in Kursk. Walking to church on Sunday was about the furthest she herself was allowed to get. Reading her novels, she had sometimes dreamed of following the man she loved, on foot if necessary, out to Siberia to share the exile to which he had been unjustly condemned, but …

'It must have been very romantic,' she said irrelevantly.

'Romantic?'

'Out on the steppe.'

'Actually, we were never out on the steppe. The first bit was forest. That was the hardest part, in fact, because we had to keep well away from the road and make our way through the undergrowth. It took us ages. But we knew the guards would be looking for us.'

'Gosh, yes!' breathed Sonya.

'In fact, we were very glad to see the forest that first morning. We had walked all night and when it became light the forest was still some way ahead of us. We were afraid we'd be caught out on the plain. Besides, Methodosius and Timofei wanted to get their chains off, but they didn't want to stop until they were safe among the trees.'

'How did they get them off?' asked Sonya.

'The Artel had given Methodosius a hammer and chisel. I think they'd also worked on them before leaving. It didn't take them long. And then, well, we just carried on.'

And on and on, thought Dmitri. The journey had seemed endless. Especially that bit in the forest. They had hardly seemed to be making any progress at all. Sometimes the way had been so blocked by undergrowth as to be impenetrable. At other times they had come upon swamps and ponds and had had to make detours.

'What did you eat?' asked Sonya.

'The Artel had given us some food. After that we ate birds' eggs.'

'How exciting!'

'Raw,' said Dmitri.

Actually, in the forest it had not been so bad. It was afterwards, when they came out into the farmland, that they had felt really hungry. There were villages but they hadn't dared to go into them. Everyone there was in the pay of the Prison Administration, or else exiles themselves.

'What about the wolves?' asked Sonya enthusiastically.

'Wolves?'

'There were wolves?'

'Not as far as I know. There were mosquitoes, though. As big as bats.'

'Big as bats?' queried Vera Samsonova.

The trouble with scientists was that they were so literal.

'They hung around us in swarms. We couldn't get rid of them. It was the swamp, I suppose.'

'You didn't run into anything, well, bigger?' asked Sonya, disappointed.

'Like what?'

'Bears?' said Sonya hopefully.

The thing they had really been worried about, of course, was soldiers. There were soldiers everywhere on the Siberian road. They had tried to keep away from it, but occasionally, forced by an extra large detour, they had caught sight of it through the trees. Always there were carts; not the prison carts going out to Tiumen, but the heavy *obozes*, or transport wagons, bringing food and furs and timber products back. And always there were guards.

Whenever they had come that close they had turned away and slipped deeper into the forest. Apart from the people on the road, they never saw anyone. There must have been people in the forest, if only the people the soldiers were guarding the carts against, but they never saw anyone.

Or any living things, either, apart from the birds and the mosquitoes. After the first few days, Dmitri found the continuous forest oppressive. At first he had welcomed the refuge the trees provided, had been relieved to escape into them. But then, as day after day passed without there being a break in the foliage overhead, he began to feel that the Russian forest, like the Russian steppe, was endless. It was like walking forever through a dark tunnel. The sun filtered its light through the dark tops of the trees enough for Methodosius to steer by, but rarely enough to lighten the gloom below.

It was an enormous relief when at last they came out into open cultivated farmland and were able to leave the forest behind them. Now there were sown fields and grazing ground for the village cattle. Walking was easier. But for the first time they began to see people. Methodosius decided it was no longer safe to walk during the day. Instead, they walked at night, giving the villages a wide berth, not because of people but because of dogs, and steering now not by the sun but by the stars.

Still, though, from time to time, forced out of their way by some obstacle or other, they caught a glimpse of the convict road. It was lined now, in this open country, by a double, sometimes triple, row of giant silver birches, seventy or eighty feet in height, set close together so that their branches interlocked to give continuous cover from the fierce Siberian sun. Walking by night, they would sometimes see the trees sharp against the moonlight, running like some great wall forever across the plain.

There was no sheltering cover now, away into which they could creep. Indeed, every morning, when the sky began to lighten, Methodosius would look around anxiously for a place in which they could hide during the day. There were, of course, occasional copses, but too often they would contain cattle or goats grazing, or even little hen-houses or beehives. Close to the villages, too, there was always the risk of being found by a dog.

This close to the border, also, there were always Cossack patrols out. And it was one of these that eventually found them.

What Dmitri had said about never being on the steppe was not completely true. Some of the land where the villagers grazed their cattle had been taken out of the steppe and beyond it was the steppe itself, a sea of grass, brown at this time of the year, extending to the horizon, featureless except for the waves that the wind sent rippling over it. In many parts it was head-high and one morning, lacking other cover, they had crept into it to hide. They had come upon a shallow pond where Methodosius had hoped to find fish. They hadn't, but there had been water birds in plenty. They hadn't eaten for days and Methodosius had decided, exceptionally, to kill a bird and cook it over a fire. It was, perhaps, the fire that gave them away.

The patrol came out of the long grass, a dozen of them, riding in line abreast. Methodosius jumped to his feet and made as if to run off, but it was already too late. The Cossacks had long whips which they simply span about him. The others froze on the spot.

The sergeant rode up to them.

'What have we here?' he said.

He looked Methodosius all over.

'Have I seen you before?' he asked.

'Me, I'm saying nothing,' said Methodosius.

'Ask him what his name is,' said the sergeant, 'and do you know what he'll say?'

'I don't remember,' said Methodosius.

'That's right. I've met your sort before.'

He looked at Timofei.

'You're not a Wanderer, though, are you? More like a Schismatic. You wouldn't be a Milk-Drinker, by any chance?'

'I am a Milk-Drinker,' said Timofei quietly.

'Breaking the law again? There's no stopping you people. Well, at least you're not likely to give us any trouble. What about you, though?' he said, looking at Dmitri.

Dmitri stayed silent.

'A political, I'd say, to look at you. Though I don't know. I don't know quite what to make of you.'

He shook his head and then turned to Anna Semeonova.

'I know what to make of you, though, love. Like to come into the grass?'

'You cut that out!' said Dmitri.

'No blows!' cried Timofei, running forward.

'He *is* a Milk-Drinker, then!' said the sergeant.

He caught Dmitri a little flick with his whip.

'And you're a trouble-maker, are you?'

'I'm a lawyer,' said Dmitri, 'and I am returning to Kursk with my client. I have my papers with me.'

'Like this?' said the Cossack. Nevertheless he dismounted from his horse and held out his hand for the papers.

He read them slowly.

'So who do you reckon you are, then?' he said, eyeing Dmitri.

'Kameron. Examining Magistrate to the Court of Kursk.'

'And she,' said the Cossack, 'would be …?'

'I am Anna Semeonova.'

The Cossack looked at the papers again.

'Stolen,' he said dismissively. He was uncertain enough, however, to give the papers back to Dmitri.

And to take them, not to Tiumen, but to Ekaterinburg.

'Boss,' said the sergeant, standing outside the door of the Chief of Police's office at Ekaterinburg, 'we've got visitors for you.'

The 'Boss' was purely honorific. The Chief of Police was not the sergeant's boss. The Cossacks came under the Exile Administration. They were, however, inclined to refer to anyone who occupied an office as 'Boss'. That didn't mean that they didn't despise them.

'Bring them in, then,' said a voice which sounded vaguely familiar.

The Chief of Police was bent over a filing cabinet with his back towards them.

'Well?' he said, without looking at them.

'We picked them up over by Virgonsk. We think they were running away.'

'Why not run them back, then?'

The sergeant hesitated.

'Boss, it may not be that straightforward. They've got papers.'

'Show me them.'

The Chief of Police turned. His jaw dropped.

'My God!' he said.

It was Novikov, ex-Chief of Police at Kursk.

'But what are you doing here?' asked Dmitri.

'I was posted here,' said Novikov, unable to keep his eyes off Anna Semeonova. 'After the unfortunate disappearance of …'

He pulled himself together.

'But, my dear Anna Semeonova!' he said. 'Such a pleasure!' He bent over her hand. 'You'll take some tea, of course? And cakes? Get some cakes, you fool!' he said to someone in an inner room. 'And tea! And – and some vodka. I rather think I need some vodka.'

'What's all this?' said the Cossack, bewildered. 'Cakes?'

'Off you go!' said Novikov, pushing him towards the door. 'Off you go! Quick! There's been some dreadful mistake.'

'Mistake?' said the Cossack. 'Right, I'll be off then. At once!'

They heard his boots clattering down the stairs.

'My dear Anna Semeonova! So pleased to see you! How is your father? And Dmitri Alexandrovich, too! Such a pleasure!' He shook Dmitri's hand warmly. 'And' – more doubtfully 0 'these two gentlemen …'

'They have been helping me in my inquiries.'

'Quite so. Delighted to meet you, gentlemen! Some tea, perhaps?'

'Did I hear someone say vodka?' asked Methodosius.

Novikov produced a bottle from his filing cabinet and then, with a shaking hand, filled glasses.

'For you, sir?' he said, turning to Timofei.

'He would prefer milk,' said Anna Semeonova.

'Ah, yes. Milk. And tea. And vodka. And – and cakes.'

'I would like to sit down,' said Anna Semeonova.

Some time later Novikov rose, a trifle unsteadily, to his feet.

'Dmitri Alexandrovich! Sir, a toast! To your continued success in your profession!'

He drained the glass, tossed it over his shoulder, then clasped Dmitri warmly to his bosom.

'My dear sir! I must congratulate you. This is really almost too much for me! To be there at the start, almost, one might say, to assist in the start, of a great career! Really ...'

He wiped his eyes and opened his arms again.

'But I have to say, it is no surprise to me. Right from your first day I said to myself: "This young man will go far!" I said so to Peter Ivanovich, too. "Your Honour," I said, "this man will go far! Such a mind! Oh," I said, "they may be able to pull the wool over our eyes, but they won't be able to do that with Dmitri Alexandrovich!" And I was right, wasn't I? You were the one who worked it out. That Shumin! I don't know what they were doing at the door to let a woman like that, a notorious terrorist, walk straight out. And, all the time, my poor, dear Anna Semeonova ...'

He burst into tears.

'If only I had known, my dear! If only I had guessed! But it took someone sharp like Dmitri Alexandrovich to see – and I, I, fool that I was, let that dear, dear girl go into exile when I would have given my heart – '

'It wasn't your fault,' said Anna Semeonova.

'Not my fault!' said Novikov. 'Oh, my precious one, you don't know what good it does me to hear you say that! Say it again, say it again, please!'

'It really wasn't your fault – '

'Oh, my dear!' Novikov fell on his knees before her. 'You will say that, won't you, back in Kursk? To your father? To his friends?

Even – yes, perhaps – to Prince Dolgorukov? And then one day – one day, maybe, just possibly – I won't have to stay in this awful place any longer? It wasn't my fault, you know, it wasn't my fault. You will say that, won't you?'

'I will,' said Anna Semeonova kindly.

'Oh, blessed one!' He seized her hand and kissed it. 'Tell them that I helped you, that I would have helped you – oh, if I could only help you!'

'Well, as a matter of fact …' said Dmitri.

Methodosius climbed gingerly up into the train.

'They didn't have these when I was here before,' he said.

He and Timofei sat uncomfortably on the edge of their seats.

After a while, Methodosius clutched at his stomach.

'Barin,' he said – he had taken to calling Dmitri "Barin," much to Dmitri's irritation – 'I feel sick.'

Dmitri and Timofei took him to the end of the coach, where there was a little platform. Afterwards, he returned to his seat and sat there pale and uneasy.

At the next stop he and Timofei climbed down and walked about a little. When the train restarted they were nowhere to be found. Imagining they had boarded the train somewhere else, Dmitri walked the length of the train searching for them.

'Perhaps it's better like this,' said Anna Semeonova. She was silent for a moment. 'Perhaps it would be better for me, too,' she said to herself, almost in a whisper.

Perm was the city where the railway stage ended. It was also the city where Dmitri had had his brush with the Chief of Police. He brushed again.

'Yes, your papers are all right,' said the Chief of Police. 'But what about hers?'

'She is the woman referred to.'

'Yes, but that doesn't mean she can travel without papers. Where have her papers got to?'

185

'Such papers as she had are with the authorities at Tiumen,' said Dmitri patiently.

'Tiumen? I don't like the sound of that! Is she a convict or something?'

'If you read the papers again,' said Dmitri, with heroic self-command, 'you will see that she is not a convict but an innocent person wrongly transported.'

'Yes, but she should still have papers. There ought to be papers of release. Otherwise she might be anyone, mightn't she?'

She might, indeed.

Dmitri did everything he could to persuade the Chief of Police, but without success. The papers had to be sent for from Tiumen. The most he was able to achieve was that while they were waiting for them Anna Semeonova could be lodged in a hotel the same hotel as Dmitri.

The same hotel as it happened, as judges used when they were on circuit in the remoter wastes of the border country. Such cities as there were did not merit a judge of their own and the province's judges were perpetually travelling.

As Dmitri and Anna Semeonova went into the dining room the following morning, Dmitri heard a voice which sounded vaguely familiar. It was taking issue with the waiter.

'Haven't you anything else?'

'Cabbage soup?' suggested the waiter hopefully.

'No, thank you.'

'Beetroot?'

'Haven't you anything which is, well, less traditional?'

'Fish soup?'

'What sort of fish?'

The waiter scratched his head.

'Well, the usual sort.'

'Perhaps I'll go straight to the second course,' said the judge. 'Now – '

He looked up and saw Dmitri and Anna Semeonova. His jaw dropped.

It was Peter Ivanovich, former Presiding Judge at the Court of Kursk.

'But, my dear fellow, my dear young lady!'

'What are you doing here?' asked Dmitri.

'I was transferred here. After that unfortunate incident involving – '

He couldn't take his eyes off Anna Semeonova.

'But this is wonderful news!' he cried, recovering swiftly. Swift recovery had always been something that Peter Ivanovich had prided himself on. Lately he had feared that the capacity was going.

'Now, I really must insist! Please, please! I will not take "no" for an answer. You really must join me. Waiter! Champagne! One, two – no, three bottles!'

After the first he took Anna Semeonova by the hand.

'My dear!' he said fondly. 'How good it is to see you! And to see you looking so well! A trifle thinner, perhaps? What is the food like in … in … Where did you say the place was? Well, it can't be worse than here. And now you are on your way home? Well, remember me to your father. Yes, yes!' cried Peter Ivanovich, suddenly lighting up. 'Remember me to your father! Do, do! Say that my dearest memories – my fondest hope – yes, my fondest hope would be to see his darling daughter restored again to the bosom of her family, yes, yes, to actually see it! See Kursk again, the blessed dome of the church, those hideous carvings on the front of the Court House – oh, if only!'

'You wouldn't care to do something for us, would you?' said Dmitri.

Dmitri had hoped to take advantage of the shining hour, at least so far as Anna Semeonova was concerned, during the long journey back up the Volga. Anna Semeonova had withdrawn into herself, however.

'There are some things I've got to think about,' she said pointedly.

There were some things Dmitri had to think about, too; and a few more when at last the boat docked at Nizhni Novgorod. Men from the Ministry of the Interior were checking the papers of everyone as they disembarked. When they came to Dmitri's and Anna Semeonova's, they looked puzzled and went away for private confabulation. Then they called them aside.

'They won't do,' they said.

'Won't do?' said Dmitri. He took the paper that Peter Ivanovich had signed only a few days before back at Perm and waved it under their noses. 'Look! Signed by a judge! Official release by the Ministry of Justice!'

'Ah, but that's the Ministry of Justice.'

'Well?'

'We're Ministry of Interior. It's got to be signed by us.'

'Well bloody sign it then!'

'Can't do that. It's got to be done by someone senior.'

Dmitri fumed.

'In any case …'

They were looking at his papers now.

'It's funny, isn't it?' one of them said to the other.

The other shrugged.

'Well, he's the one to sort it out!'

Dmitri and Anna Semeonova were taken not to the police station that Dmitri had visited before but to an altogether grander building. Ministry of Interior guards clustered at the entrance and were spread about the corridors inside. Two of them took Dmitri and Anna Semeonova up some stairs and along to a room with huge, imposing doors. They entered a small ante room with a door on the other side. One of the guards tapped discreetly and went in.

'Bring them in!' said a voice which Dmitri couldn't quite place but which sounded –

Inside, a man was sitting at a large desk with his head bent over some papers. He looked up.

'Good God!' he said.

It was Porfiri Porfirovich, late President of the Special Tribunal at the Court of Kursk.

'But I didn't expect you to come back!' said Porfiri Porfirovich.

'Well, thanks,' said Dmitri.

'I didn't imagine for one moment ...' His shocked eyes took in Anna Semeonova. 'Is this the young lady? You found her? And brought her back? Here?'

He buried his face in his hands.

'What am I going to do? What *am* I going to do?'

'Do?' said Dmitri.

'Well, I can't just let you go, can I? Let you go back to Kursk? It would all come out. The whole thing! It would reflect so badly on the Ministry, on – on the system, on *everything*!'

'You're not going to send us back to Tiumen!' said Anna Semeonova, stunned.

'We-ell ...'

Dmitri leaned forward.

'Porfiri Porfirovich, are you happy here?'

'Happy? In Nizhni Novgorod?'

'This is your chance,' said Dmitri.

13

When they got back to Kursk, the first thing Dmitri did was to write two reports.

In the first one he gave an account of his search for Anna Semeonova, described the difficulties he had faced, and made recommendations. Some of the recommendations were actually implemented and the report as a whole was officially welcomed. Since Anna Semeonova was now restored to the bosom of her family, and since, in the view of many, she had largely brought the whole thing on herself, not much further action seemed necessary. Those unfortunate enough to be caught with the responsibility – Porfiri Porfirovich, Peter Ivanovich and Novikov – had already been transferred, which was probably punishment too much. Dmitri did put in a word for them and in the course of time they were moved a few hundred miles nearer St Petersburg. On the whole, though, all parties – Anna Semeonova's family, Anna Semeonova her slightly shamefaced self, and certainly the authorities – felt that the affair should be allowed to die as quickly as possible.

Anna Semeonova's parents proposed to take her abroad.

'You need a good holiday,' they said.

But Anna Semeonova didn't want a holiday. She wanted to testify, she said.

In his second report, Dmitri described the incident in the forest, gave the names of those concerned, listed his evidence and cited witnesses. He sent the report directly to the Minister of Justice.

After a while, when he heard nothing, he asked to see the Minister. A little unexpectedly – for he had expected to be fobbed off with underlings – an appointment was speedily made with the Minister himself.

The Minister welcomed him warmly.

'A good piece of work!' he said approvingly. 'On your part, at least.'

'There will be a Public Inquiry, then?'

'Oh, I wouldn't go so far as to say that! An inquiry, certainly. I have raised the matter with my colleague, the Minister of the Interior, and he has promised to look into it.'

'You have sent him my report?'

'I have sent him extracts from your report. In years to come, you may be thankful for this.'

'But the Ministry will do nothing!'

'Oh, no, it will do something. Judging from your report, mistakes have been made. It will want to look into these, alter its procedures, perhaps, reprimand those concerned ...'

'Reprimand?' said Dmitri. 'Not try?'

The Minister hesitated.

'I think you know the position,' he said. 'The Ministry of the Interior is, in a sense, a law unto itself. Its actions and its officers are regulated by administrative process, under the Special Provisions. I have no power to intervene.'

'There can be no recourse to the courts?'

'Unless the Tsar so decrees.'

'They can get away with murder!' said Dmitri.

'I am afraid', said the Minister, 'that they can.'

He held out his hand.

'Your work has not been in vain,' he said. 'It has been noticed. I think you will go far in your career. Provided, of course, you keep within the necessary limits.'

'So – so what's going to happen?'

'Nothing,' replied the Minister.

'Nothing!' said Vera Samsonova, outraged.

'That's what he said.'

'But what do *you* say, Dmitri? What do *you* say?'

'I don't know.'

'You're not going to let it rest?'

'I don't want to. But for the moment I can't see what else I can do.'

'You must publish it to the world!' cried Igor Stepanovich.

'Yes, but how? If I send it to the newspapers they won't print it. If they did try to print it, the Ministry censors would stop them.'

'Perhaps you could go round telling everybody?' said Igor Stepanovich.

'I've told you,' said Dmitri, irritated. 'Will that do?'

'Of course it won't!' snapped Vera Samsonova. 'I know what you mean, Dmitri, but surely there is some way in which we can influence public opinion?'

'An underground pamphlet?' suggested Igor.

'That would get *us* sent to Siberia!' said Sonya's brother, Pavel.

'Public meetings?'

'The police would close them down.'

'Surely there must be *something* we could do!' said Vera Samsonova, frowning in thought.

There was a long silence.

'I know!' said Sonya suddenly. 'I'll get my parents to take me abroad for a holiday.'

'Well, that's very nice,' said Dmitri, 'but – '

'No, don't you see? We can't publish *in* Russia, but we can publish *out* of Russia. I'll take your report with me, Dmitri, lots of copies. And then I'll send them to the newspapers over there.'

'I like that,' said Vera Samsonova.

'I'll ask my parents tonight. I'll tell them that all this dreadful business about Anna Semeonova has quite upset me. You can come too,' she said to her brother. 'Oh, and you'll have to help me copy the report. I can't do it all myself.'

'We'll *all* help,' said Vera Samsonova.

'You don't need to copy the entire report,' said Dmitri. 'Extracts will do.'

Events then moved faster than he had expected. Only a month or so later he was called to St Petersburg.

'My dear boy!' said Prince Dolgorukov. 'So pleased to see you! Don't I know your father?'

'I doubt it,' said Dmitri. 'He's dead.'

Dolgorukov gave him a puzzled look.

'That's odd,' he said. 'Kameron is such an unusual name. I'm sure I know someone …'

'My grandfather, perhaps?'

'A somewhat irascible old gentleman?'

'That's him.'

'Of course! I remember now. Alexander Dmitrovich. We were at gymnasium together. And did he not serve …?'

'On his Zemstvo.'

'Wasn't there some question about land?'

'There was.'

'I remember! Well, he was always independent-minded.' He looked sternly at Dmitri. 'But loyal to the Tsar!'

'Loyal to the Tsar,' said Dmitri, 'but independent-minded.'

The Prince looked at him again.

'Now,' he said, 'about this report of yours. Word appears to have got out.'

'Really?'

'Extracts have appeared in newspapers abroad.'

'Astonishing!'

'You have no idea how that came about, I suppose?'

'Someone inside the Ministry of the Interior?'

Dolgorukov smiled.

'Well, maybe we don't need to go into it. Just at the moment. The fact is, it *has* come out. And so we must decide what we're going to do about it.'

'Are you asking me as a lawyer?'

'Why not?'

'I suggest you bring those responsible to trial.'

The Prince shook his head.

'As a lawyer you must know that the Courts have no jurisdiction over what goes on in Siberia.'

'But – '

'It could happen only if the Tsar decreed that it should. And I'm not sure he would be willing to do that. It would amount almost to a waiving of prerogative. I doubt if the Tsar's advisers, let alone His Majesty himself, would wish to go so far. Even in such a heinous case as this.'

'You admit that it's heinous?'

'Oh, yes.'

'Well, then,' said Dmitri, 'what are you going to do?'

The Prince hesitated.

'Ordinarily, I would do nothing. Nothing is usually the most sensible thing to do, and in anything involving the Ministry of the Interior it is almost invariably the wisest policy. But ...'

'But?' said Dmitri.

'In this case that option may no longer be open to us. The Tsar is shortly to visit Berlin and Paris and questions are sure to be asked – they manage their press rather less well than we do. We don't want His Majesty to be embarrassed. So, well, although ordinarily, as I say, I would do nothing, on this occasion, in these particular circumstances, the announcement of a Public Inquiry might prove very timely ...'

Anna Semeonova's willingness to give evidence was crucial. It was also, her mother pointed out, unladylike. Anna Semeonova had been a great disappointment to her parents altogether since she had returned home. They had been confident that after her terrible adventures – terrible adventures they must have been, although they did not like to inquire too closely – she would be only too glad to return to the life she had led before that dreadful thing had happened to her in the Court House at Kursk. Far from it, they found that they had a new daughter who was, well, not exactly wild but definitely less tractable than she had been.

'Give her time!' counselled the family doctor sagely, and prescribed laudanum, which, on the advice of Vera Samsonova, Anna threw away.

She was seeing quite a lot of Vera, calling on her at the dispensary almost every day. Her parents were not best pleased, feeling that Vera was in some obscure way partly to blame for the whole thing. Her father ventured a mild objection but was told in no uncertain terms that in future Anna meant to see exactly whom she liked. Moreover, she intended to take up an appointment as assistant in the dispensary the day the inquiry was over: the better, she said, to prepare herself for the training as a doctor which she intended shortly to undertake.

Her parents consulted the family doctor once more and he again prescribed laudanum, for them this time. He also pointed out that under the recent educational reforms the opportunities for women to go to university had been greatly restricted, and that if Anna Semeonova wished to study medicine it would now have to be abroad.

'That's right,' said Anna. 'Leipzig.'

With her hopes crashing around her, Anna's mother turned desperately to Dmitri.

'Dear Dmitri Alexandrovich,' she cooed, 'we had so hoped that you and Anna – '

'Definitely not!' said Dmitri.

Not, too, said Anna Semeonova, even more definitely.

The fact was that Dmitri was disappointed by Anna Semeonova. He had hoped that her experiences would have cured her forever of her dogooding desires.

'But what is this I hear?' he said to Vera Samsonova. 'She wants to become a doctor!'

'She will be very well suited to it,' said Vera Samsonova, 'especially now that she has had some practical experience. All that was holding her back was that she felt she wasn't as clever as other people. A feeling that, now that she has met you, my dear Dmitri, she has lost.'

The fact was, though, too, that Dmitri was himself a little uncertain as to the direction his career should take. He had no illusions about his popularity in official circles and thought it likely that once the inquiry was over, the trajectory of his career was likely to be a flat one, at least so far as government service was concerned. But he had in any case been doing some of that reading that he had promised himself while in Tiumen and was no longer certain that a Tsar's lawyer was what he wanted to be.

Was it possible to be any other kind of lawyer? He went to St Petersburg and spoke to a lawyer who had represented the defendants on one of the few occasions when the Government had been misguided enough to bring a prosecution in the public courts against political dissidents. The man listened carefully.

'Yes,' he said, 'you could practise privately, and we would be glad to have you. But are you sure it is the right thing to do? If you really want to change the legal system, the only way in which you have a chance of succeeding is by working from inside.

Believe me, I know, because I have spent a lifetime trying to change it from the outside.'

But to Dmitri, at that time, continuing in Government service seemed a fate worse than death, and he was on the point of sending in his resignation when Prince Dolgorukov, of all people, sowed a seed of doubt in his mind.

He had summoned Dmitri to tell him that now that the inquiry had published its findings, the Government was proceeding to a public trial.

'Hardly necessary, in my view,' he said, shrugging his shoulders, 'but the Tsar was made to feel, while he was abroad, that something of the sort was required. The Prosecution's case, will, of course, be based on your report. Actually, it works out rather well, for the Tsar will be able to say that intervention from abroad is quite unnecessary as the matter was already in hand thanks to the vigilance of his law officers. It works out rather well for you, too, of course. A promising career beckons.'

'Does it?' said Dmitri sceptically.

Dolgorukov stared at him.

'Oh, yes. If you're going to have a system at all, you might as well have intelligent people running it.'

'I'm not so sure about the system,' said Dmitri.

'There's always room for improvement, no doubt,' said Prince Dolgorukov.

The issue was much discussed by the small circle of friends at Kursk.

'What do you think, Vera?' asked Sonya one day as they sat helping Anna Semeonova to do her embroidery. 'What will Dmitri choose?'

'Career or career?' said Vera.

'I don't think that's very kind of you, Vera,' said Sonya reproachfully.

It was the last day on which they would all be able to be together. The trial had just come to a satisfactory conclusion and the next day Anna Semeonova was going on holiday. She had at last agreed, somewhat to her parents' surprise, stipulating only that the holiday should be in Samara. Apparently it was possible to take a milk-drinking cure there. Her parents were relieved to find her at last doing something so safely fashionable.

Dmitri was on his way to the house to wish her a safe journey when he was accosted by a rough-looking figure. The man thrust a large packet into his hands and made off. Opening it, Dmitri found a wad of hundred-rouble notes, together with a grimy slip of paper, which said:

'Your fee. The Artel.'

KILLER READS

DISCOVER THE BEST
IN CRIME AND THRILLER

Follow us on social media to get to know the team behind the books, enter exclusive giveaways, learn about the latest competitions, hear from our authors, and lots more:

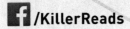 /KillerReads

 /KillerReads